BOUND
BY
PROPHECY

DESCENDANTS SERIES

BOUND
BY
PROPHECY

MELISSA WRIGHT

Bound by Prophecy
Copyright © 2013 by Melissa Wright

All rights reserved. No part of this book may be used or reproduced in any manner whatsoever including Internet usage, without written permission of the author.

This is a work of fiction. The names, characters, places, or events used in this book are the product of the author's imagination or used fictitiously. Any resemblance to actual people, alive or deceased, events or locales is completely coincidental.

Book design by Maureen Cutajar
www.gopublished.com

ISBN-10: 1484067894
ISBN-13: 978-1484067895

For thousands of years, the Seven Lines have held a prophecy. The details are vague, as such things often are, but it can pretty much be summed up like this: Do things right, or everyone will die.

1

THE GIRL

They called it a thinning of the blood. Though most of our ancestors' magic had slowly weakened, it still left us the ability to hold sway over humans. I glanced around the room where I hung chained by the ankles. *Damn sight of good it's doing me now*, I thought.

"Aern," my brother asked coolly, "where did you hide the girl?"

I glanced at the abandoned warehouse's walls. The concrete floor. There really was no way out.

Morgan stepped closer, plainly irritated he had neither my answer nor attention. "Aern." I recognized the fury in his tone, though he tried to mask it. He was a lean man, only an inch or so shorter than I, but he was strong. Not only his body, but his mind, the power to control any human he touched. He was stronger than the rest of us, and that was why he needed her.

I finally looked at my brother.

"The girl," he demanded.

He looked odd from this perspective. His custom-tailored suit, his Italian loafers, all of it wrong now. I tilted my head to see him better. Maybe it was just the blood rushing to my brain.

"Have you lost weight, brother?" I asked. "You seem thin."

Morgan's jaw went tight, his nostrils flared the tiniest bit.

I smiled, though my cheeks throbbed with the effort. I could feel the blood vessels expanding at my neck and temples. "Must be the stress," I said.

He shifted. "Tell me or I will flay you."

"You should try yoga," I offered. "It's very soothing."

He took another step forward, doing his best to control the angry glare that wanted to take over his chiseled features.

My ears began to pound.

"Brother"—he reached out a finger and pushed and my body began to swing slowly—"you will not escape with her."

The low thrum began to pulse through my entire body. I relaxed my head back as I hung, still swaying from the push. I wasn't certain how much longer I could stay like this.

Morgan lifted the lapel of his jacket with one hand and gracefully removed a thin silver dagger from an inside pocket with the other. He let me stare at it for a long moment before he whispered, "Is she worth it?"

"You and I both know you can draw and quarter me right here," I said. "But you will get nothing."

Morgan smiled. "You can't even say her name, can you?"

"You will get nothing," I repeated.

Suddenly, a heavy warehouse door slammed against the metal siding as it was thrown open. Morgan was within striking distance and I took the chance, the only one I was likely to get.

As his head swiveled to find the source of the noise, mine swung forward full force and connected with the bridge of his nose. His eyes narrowed on me as tears welled up and blood began to stream over his lip.

My blood pounded and ears rang, but I didn't hear movement from the intruder, only the distant wail of sirens.

Morgan watched me for a heartbeat before sliding the dagger back into his breast pocket. His mouth turned up in a triumphant smile one instant, and then he was running past me the next.

I tried to turn to see where he'd gone, out some back entrance apparently, but I had limited mobility, suspended as I was. When I swung back to straight, there was a face inches from mine. I admit I may have jumped, if only a little.

"Where is my sister?" she hissed.

Under normal circumstances, my mouth might have fallen open.

She smacked me. "My sister. What did you do to her?"

I shook my head. Glanced at the chain hoist that attached my harness to the warehouse wall. "No," I started, but the girl wasn't looking at me now. She was watching the door.

The sirens were getting closer. And something else, a muffled buzzing.

"They're coming here?" I asked.

The girl turned back to me, nodded. I was struggling to find my focus, to sway her to co-operate. She seemed a bit panicked, but for the wrong reasons.

"Here." I tilted my head up to indicate my bindings. "Untie me. I will help you find her."

Her eyes narrowed and her mouth screwed up as she considered my proposition.

The sirens were at the gate.

"Two minutes," I warned. "It's the only way you'll find her."

Car doors slammed. She knew I was right.

I had her.

And then she was gone. "Wait," I shouted, "where are you going?"

She didn't look back as she ran across the open floor. She moved with such unrestrained fervor, I half expected her to slam into the wall. As she reached up, she pulled a screwdriver from her back jeans pocket, and pried the lever that held my chain.

An instant later, I slammed into the concrete floor.

Fire spread through my shoulder, but the pounding in my head was replaced with the reverberations of a small, clanging bell. Tingling prickled my limbs a moment before I realized my feet were being jerked, and the twinkling lights flashing against blackness were the first indication to my brain that I couldn't see anything. The tingle turned to pinpricks and the ringing in my ears quieted as I tried to bat my eyelids open.

The jerking at my feet ceased.

"Can you stand?"

The face was in my line of sight again, this time sideways.

"Gll…tthhh," I answered.

She grimaced.

The girl reached down to grab my arm, and the fire increased tenfold. I said something like, "Aaaaah," and she let go.

Apparently, I'd managed to keep from busting my skull against concrete by shifting my head sideways during the fall, but had taken the brunt of the hit on my shoulder, which was likely now broken.

The girl was pulling up on my other side. "Come on," she hissed, "we have to go."

Two deep male voices echoed off the exterior walls of the warehouse.

"Now."

She yanked hard against me, and eventually my instincts kicked in. Or at least adrenaline. I was up, nearly falling forward before being pulled behind her toward a short flight of metal grate stairs. My right arm swung limp behind me; I was completely unable to support it since my other arm was held within her considerable grip.

As we climbed, I glanced behind us, saw a shadow through the open warehouse door, and then stumbled on the threshold of a back entrance as I was dragged into daylight.

The murky water of the bay lay only thirty yards before us, but I was abruptly jerked sideways and led down the deck through a narrow pass between two storage containers. At the end of the pass, the girl stopped dead to peer around the containers. I leaned forward, heaving in breath. Before I got two searing lungfuls, she was off again, my forearm firmly in her grasp.

I was about to complain, or free myself to lie down, when she slid into a shed.

She pushed me down beneath a boarded window, and I leaned back against the shed wall, half hidden from view of the door as she held it open a fraction of an inch to watch for our would-be pursuers.

It was dim in the shed, and the thin line of light put most of her in shadow. I looked away, quickly surveying our surroundings. An unused maintenance shed, shelves now empty of anything of worth. Dust silhouettes decorated the walls, outlining empty nails that once held pliers and wrenches and spools. A few lengths of wire scattered the floor, along with years-old paper and trash.

I was sure there was something I could use to fashion a sling for my arm, a way to take the strain off my shoulder, but my eyes were back on the girl.

Light filtered through the soft curls of her hair, making the color, somewhere between dark blonde and light brown, appear golden. Her features were petite, aside from her lips, which seemed maybe too full from this vantage point. She was remarkably familiar, and yet, inexplicably, unfamiliar. It was impossible to see her eyes, narrowed on her task as they were.

Her shoulders rose and fell in a way that said she was trying to be quiet, but needed breath as much as I.

A metallic sound echoed in the distance and she pushed the door shut. When she turned, her hands waved frantically in a gesture meant to shoo me farther back and out of view. I felt my mouth quirk at her actions, but any humor instantly fell away when I shifted and pain seared my neck and shoulder anew.

Farther back, I leaned once more against the shed wall.

A missing slat in the half wall protecting me gave me a view of the opposite wall, where the girl had flattened herself against it between a cabinet and a hanging rack in an attempt to hide. She was unaware I watched her.

Two voices floated over us, their direction hard to discern as they reverberated off metal sheds and containers outside. The girl held impossibly still—I couldn't even be certain she was breathing. My gaze narrowed on her as I attempted to better see in the darkness.

Her lips were moving, and I found myself leaning forward to read them. Was she praying?

The shed door swung open and I froze, holding my breath.

I could approach the man, probably should. I could sway him into letting me go and detaining the girl.

But I wasn't confident I'd succeed. Not simply because the officer would be difficult to touch, nor the fact that he would likely hold me at a distance at gunpoint until the other arrived, but because something had gone wrong above the warehouse floor.

I had tried to reach the girl by sight alone, and it hadn't worked. She'd released me, yes, but she'd run across the warehouse to drop me like a sack of oats when she could have unlatched my arms as I'd asked and safely rescued me. And when I'd landed, she'd not responded to my mental requests, instead unlashing me to yank behind her like a leashed dog and then throwing me into this cubby hole in a shed.

I was afraid something was off, that something had happened when I'd hit my head.

But that wasn't all. There was another reason to stay. Something about this girl.

The door closed. The officer's footfalls moved past the shed.

He was satisfied he'd cleared the area.

The girl waited several minutes, and then moved across the shed to peek out a slit in the boarded window above me.

Her white tennis shoes came to a rest just beside my feet. The window covering shifted, and I could see her face more clearly. Not a girl exactly, maybe seventeen or eighteen years old. A shapeless jacket hung open over her faded tee shirt. Her jeans were worn, shoes scuffed.

"I think they're gone," she whispered to the window opening.

It struck me I was rather far behind with what was happening and exactly who this was. She didn't appear to be a criminal, but she *had* slapped me pretty good.

"Why are the police looking for you?" I asked.

She fell into a squat beside me. "Shhhh! What is wrong with you?"

"I thought they were gone?"

She shook her head, brushed a caramel lock from her face.

"So, why are the cops after you?" I repeated in a softer voice.

She glanced behind her, as if we weren't alone in the empty shed, and then back before answering. "They aren't." She grimaced, not wanting to admit the rest. "I couldn't figure out how you got in, so I pried the lock." Her face flushed the tiniest bit. "It set off the alarm."

That explained the buzzing. And then the "pried" registered. "The screwdriver?"

She shrugged. "You work with what you've got."

"And you were following me."

Her eyes narrowed further. "I know you have my sister. I saw you take her."

I shifted, hoping my sway would work when she decided to skewer me with a two-dollar screwdriver. And then a thought seized me, the notion that this might not be one of Morgan's plans, that she might be telling the truth, and I had to play it as such, even on the slightest chance.

"You don't understand," I said, working to keep my tone level through the pain radiating from my shoulder. "She isn't safe without me."

Her hand twitched. "You're some kind of psychopath, then." Her frown tightened. "Do you even know what you've done with her?"

I sighed. "She hasn't been harmed. I swear it."

"Prove it. Take me to her."

"I can't. It's the only way she's safe."

"Do it, or I stab you right now and call those policemen back here."

A rusty pair of shears was suddenly inches from my throat, pulled from beside the hundred-and-ten-pound girl threatening my life.

I wasn't afraid of her, exactly. But what if she was telling the truth? What if this was Brianna's sister?

"Fine," I said. "But you have to prove something to me first."

The shears moved forward, poking into the tender skin above my jugular.

"How do I know you are really her sister?"

In a flash of anger, she brought the rusty tool up and knocked a chunk of the covering loose from the window.

Light rushed in and I blinked hard against it. When I focused finally on her face, I got the first good look at her since she'd slammed open the warehouse door.

It was Brianna, but suddenly filled with fury and life. This version wasn't as thin or frail; those few pounds changed her face slightly, gave her fuller lips and healthy, rosy cheeks, but they were the same.

And those eyes. Brianna's impossibly wide, sea-glass green eyes that seemed continuously jumping between wonder and terror were narrowed on me here, at once ice and fire.

I leaned closer, my whisper of disbelief cut short by shooting pain.

I gasped, grabbing my shoulder, and then got my voice back. "Why did you drop me?"

Her mouth twisted with what might have been humor. One shoulder lifted. "I thought you'd be easier to handle this way."

I stared at her open-mouthed. This was not my Brianna.

2

DECEPTION

I was lying to her.

This poor girl was clearly Brianna's sister, and I couldn't tell her the truth. There was no way I could reunite them.

It wasn't safe.

"Emily," I said, coming to a standstill despite the insistent tugging on my arm. "Where are you dragging me?"

Her brows dropped, unbelievably, lower. After a long, uncomfortably silent wait in the shed, she'd decided the policemen were no longer a threat and gone ahead with her mission, pulling me up from the floor to follow her through the maze of containers and outbuildings surrounding the warehouse. Her mood had decidedly not improved after my capture.

"I have to get my bag," she explained, "and I can't very well trust you not to run off, now can I?"

There was no accounting for the way her anger consistently caused the corner of my mouth to twitch, but I bit down against it. Her tone made everything she hadn't said perfectly clear. I was a psychopathic kidnapper. No two ways about it.

She pulled forward again, and then, two steps later, came to an abrupt halt. I started to question the pause when she spun on me, her chest heaving long, angry breaths.

When she at last spoke, she punctuated each word. "How. Did. You. Know. My. Name?"

My lips pursed. I knew better than to answer.

I hadn't actually known the name was hers. It had only been whispered in sleep, loosed in restless sobbing. I had assumed the name belonged to the girl's mother. But I'd not known she had a twin. I hadn't understood.

She stared fire at me.

"Your sister," I finally answered. "Brianna."

Her face twisted at the words, and I felt a sudden stab of guilt. I was protecting her, I reminded myself. Protecting us all. This was the only way.

And then she hauled off and punched me.

It might not have hurt if I wasn't sporting a broken shoulder. I automatically gripped my arm at the elbow to support the injury, and cursed. For one brief instant, I considered leaving her. Touching her face, dropping her into a coma, and walking away.

But I couldn't. Morgan would find her. Use her.

We stared at each other for a long moment, both of us knowing there was no other way.

And then she grabbed my arm again, yanking even harder as she tugged me behind her.

We passed the side entrance I'd used when spying on Morgan. *Before I got caught*, I thought bitterly, and it steeled my resolve. I had to help this girl. If for no other reason, Morgan could use her against Brianna.

Emily let go of my arm as we came to a pair of trash dumpsters, and slipped into the narrow space between the two. The smell was rancid, as if somehow this empty warehouse churned out fish guts instead of lawn furniture. And then I remembered even the furniture hadn't been produced here in years. The metal scraps that littered the yard were aged, rusting.

So Morgan's goons were using these buildings for something. Something that reeked of death. My eyes narrowed on the dumpster's lid.

"Are you having an episode or something?" Emily snapped as she reappeared inches from me. "Is this part of your 'condition'?"

I didn't open the lid, which was probably a good thing, since this angry young woman would no doubt think I was responsible for whatever lay inside.

"You have your bag," I said levelly. "What now?"

She shrugged the duffle bag further up her shoulder. Concentrated for a moment. Screwed up her mouth. "I don't suppose you have a car or something nearby?"

"No, I don't suppose I do."

Her shoulder rose and fell in a sigh. "Well, then I guess we walk back."

She turned to go and I reached up to stop her. The instant my hand touched her left shoulder, the bag dropped from her right and she spun to strike me.

"Whoa," I said, throwing my hands up. "Easy."

Her jaw tightened. "Don't touch me."

I resisted the urge to bring up the dozen or so times she'd had a hold of me since we'd met. "Fine," I answered. I waited a moment for her to calm. "What do you mean 'back?'"

Her face relaxed to confusion. "Back to the house where I found you." She pointed absently toward the east. "My car is parked in an alley two blocks down."

I automatically stepped forward to grasp her arms, to shake her, and had to restrain myself. "No. You can't go back there. You can never go back there."

She opened her mouth, the words 'my car' silently forming through her shock at my vehemence.

"Forget the car. It's lost to you." I shook my head, furious. "Morgan's probably already found it. His minions have probably sniffed out every clue in it. The registration, it'll have your address, your name. They'll know. They've got us now."

"Seriously," Emily said, "do we need to get your medication or something?"

I threw my hands up, and then stopped short when the pain cut through my shoulder anew. "Aaaaahhhh!"

Emily leaned back, suddenly leery instead of determined.

"I am not mentally ill," I said in as calm and even a tone as I could manage. "That... man you saw earlier, the one who chained me by the ankles"—I waited until her expression indicated she was remembering the image—"he is the insane one."

I was quiet while she let it sink in. Slowly, she began to nod. "Yes, that makes sense."

I let out a long breath, grateful I was finally getting through.

"So, you're both insane," she decided. "Did you meet in the nuthouse or is there like a club or something?"

An exasperated growl escaped me. "I'm not insane!"

A petite hand came to rest on her hip as she leaned forward again. "Oh, really? Then, why, pray tell, did you kidnap my sister?"

My palm slapped against my face and I took two long breaths before opening my eyes to peer through the fingers at her.

She waited.

I dropped my hand in defeat. "Circumstance, Emily. Circumstance."

"I don't think I believe you," she said, only a hint of a tremor in her voice. "I can't think of any circumstance that would call for you stealing Brianna."

"And I can't think of any circumstance that would call for a girl with a screwdriver to drop me from a chain to break my shoulder against a concrete floor and drag me along as if I'm some kind of hostage. But here we are." I glanced up and down the space between the buildings. "Now let's get moving before someone finds us."

She didn't speak for a blissful five minutes or so, merely walking behind me. I wasn't certain whether she'd been thinking and finally come to a decision or had just realized she'd begun to follow instead of lead when her diligent stride turned into a kind of hopping jog to overtake mine.

"Hey!" she spat when she appeared beside me. She reached out to grab my arm again, but stopped just short, narrowed her eyes, and then drew her hand to her side where it fisted against her leg. I pulled back a smile. So that was it, then. She wasn't about to let me call her on anything. Not this psycho. "Where, exactly, are we going?" she asked.

I sighed. "To find your sister."

I could see the argument forming, wanting to tear out of her, but she didn't seem entirely sure what to do.

"That's what you want, isn't it?"

She swallowed. Glanced forward, then back at me. When she spoke, it was almost a whisper. "Where is she?"

I turned my eyes ahead, toward the gates that led from the factory grounds. "Safe. That's all that matters for now."

It wasn't answer enough, but Emily was clearly too tired for quarreling. There was a darkness under her eyes and I wondered if she'd slept at all since I'd taken Brianna. And then I corrected myself, because I'd not *taken* Brianna. I'd *saved* her.

We reached the chain link fence enclosing the property and I pulled a loose section up at the base for Emily to crawl through. She eyed me suspiciously, but went under. Climbing through myself proved to be a challenge with an injured shoulder, yet I received no help from her. Or pity.

I made it, though the fence dropped with a metallic clang behind me, snapping down on my ankle. I gritted my teeth against the pain in my shoulder and yanked my foot free, but not before ripping the hem of my jeans. I looked at Emily, arms crossed as she glared down at me, and tried once more to reach her, to sway her to help me up.

"Are you coming, or what?" she snapped.

With a resigned sigh, and one good arm, I pushed to my feet.

"You sigh a lot," she said.

"I never used to," I muttered as I brushed asphalt off my pant leg. My shoulder hurt and the whole situation was making my nerves raw. My gaze met hers. "You narrow your eyes a lot."

She scowled. "Well, I only narrow my eyes at people who've kidnapped my sister."

I returned the frown. "And I only sigh when people wrongly accuse me of kidnapping their sister." I glanced down the street. "Let's go. I don't like the looks of that car."

As I stepped into the street, Emily peered at the sedan several blocks down. "Hey, um"—she hesitated when she realized she didn't know my name, and then shook her head, deciding it didn't matter—"I think I know that car."

I was running for her before I heard the engine accelerate. She'd no sooner realized it was speeding toward us than my good arm was around her waist, dragging her back from the street. But it didn't matter, it was all asphalt here. There was nothing to shield us. I ran against the fence, Emily in tow, knowing there was nowhere for us to hide, realizing I'd have to make a choice.

The property beside us was theirs. Nothing but the warehouse they'd apparently been using and could be in now. The opposite side of the road held brick-walled industrial units, abandoned and closed off. It was too far to the populated areas. Too far for any kind of shelter. If I was alone, I'd make it. But I wasn't. There was Emily. It would have to be her or me, and I wasn't even sure she could do it; I was practically dragging her as it was.

And then she was running with me, suddenly aware of the danger. I knew why. Sparks flew as the car swerved onto the sidewalk and scraped against the chain-link fence in broken shrieks. It was too close. We weren't going to make it.

We passed an electric pole and I cut left, pulling Emily with me as I ran forward across the two-lane road. I could see the sedan in my peripheral now, and as soon as it was close enough it would have to account for the pole, I cut back, running straight in the opposite direction. Its tires squealed as it spun to chase us.

The girl was fast, I'd give her that. But even I couldn't outrun a Buick.

"There." I tilted my head toward a dark alley between two buildings. "Don't stop and don't look back."

She glanced at me, but only briefly, because the car smashed into a trash bin on the roadside behind us. *Too close.* Her jacket dropped to the ground behind her as she fell into full speed. I didn't know when she'd lost the duffle bag.

As Emily's track veered right, I stayed left, an easier target for the driver. And I'd been fairly certain I was the target. Until the car sped, and raced straight for Emily.

I cursed and adjusted my path, hoping the sight of me so close to his bumper would have some effect on the driver's course. It didn't. He was going to run Emily down.

Time slowed as I watched the car advance on her, helpless. Each footfall stretched into minutes. She didn't look back, but as if she could feel she was losing ground, had only moments before it was too late, she ran impossibly faster. *Faster than me.*

But I didn't have time to process the thought, because only seconds since the chase began, the car smashed into the block corner of the building. Metal shrieked and twisted as its forward momentum pushed against the immovable wall, and time returned again.

Panting, I ran toward the mess, leaping over the smashed hood where steam billowed from the crumpled metal. The car's horn blared as the driver slumped against the steering wheel, splattered with blood and broken glass. My feet came down hard on the other side of the car, in the narrow space between the buildings. As I searched for her, my mind raced, replaying the images from the crash, what I thought I'd seen.

I had to be sure.

I numbly called her name, and then looked down the alley. She was there, two blocks down, still sprinting as she turned the corner.

I stared dumbly for a long moment before finally running after her.

When I caught her six blocks later, it was only by chance. She'd taken a wrong turn and had gotten trapped by a too-high fence. Not that she planned to let a fence stop her, because she had climbed to the top of the eight feet and was lifting her leg over as I watched, but at least it had given me the break I needed to close the distance.

"Emily," I called as I drew closer.

She looked up at me, surprised, and froze halfway across the metal bar that topped the chain link. Her chest was heaving with the exertion, but she'd somehow managed to make it.

My hands went up in a frustrated gesture and she stared down at me blankly. And then, as it dawned on her, she simply shrugged her shoulders. "You said don't stop."

I sighed and then gave her that shooing motion she'd given me in the shed before grabbing onto the fence to follow her up. I dropped to the ground beside her, surreptitiously checking her condition. It appeared she'd only skinned her palms, which left her in far better condition than I, considering what the fence climbing had done to my injured shoulder. When she saw me looking, she curled her hands into fists, though I believed it was due more to the trembling in her fingers than the scrapes on her palms.

We continued wordlessly out of the industrial area at a jog. I was surprised she could maintain the pace after what she'd been through, but I refrained from questioning her just yet. We wouldn't be safe until we'd gotten locked inside somewhere.

We kept jogging, past the now-empty apartments that had once housed the industrial workers. It didn't feel safe, not yet. I didn't stop until we reached the edge of downtown, the parking garages and empty alleys that would be crowded on a weekday. Emily didn't appear too keen on running down another alley, but she didn't argue, simply keeping pace beside me until I ducked behind a low bin that would allow me to see in both directions.

Panting, we leaned against the brick wall of an old building, struggling viciously to catch our breath. Emily wheezed and bent over to brace her hands on her knees. Our chests heaved, pulses still racing, limbs tingling and weak. I was certain she'd slide down to the pavement if not for the filth that lined the alley. I'd no idea how far we'd run, but we had farther to go if I were to keep us safe. I glanced at the girl beside me, baggy tee shirt draped as she leaned against herself and the wall, hair a mess of damp curls and loose waves shifting in the breeze.

Morgan had targeted her, not me. He'd known he needed to keep me alive if he wanted to find Brianna, so he'd used her. He'd run from the warehouse and set that human after Emily. To prove a point? To hurt me? It didn't matter. He'd tried to kill her. He *had* killed the driver of that car.

The image of the sedan smashing into bricks, nearly grazing Emily as she ran, replayed in my mind and I cursed.

She looked up, still panting. "Okay." She swallowed hard against her parched throat. "I'll play along." She wagged a finger vaguely in the direction of the incident, now miles away. "Who was that?"

I waved away her concern. "Just a commonblood. Morgan's not wasting any of his men on this."

Her brow raised in utter disbelief.

"That's good news," I explained. "If they want to kill you, then they haven't found the car, haven't figured out who you are yet."

She straightened, but it was only to lean back. Away from me. And then I winced as I realized how it all must have sounded to her.

I didn't know how to make her understand, so I didn't try. "I'm sorry," I said. "But Brianna is safe, I promise you that."

At the mention of Brianna, something changed in Emily. Her breathing steadied and she became remarkably still.

Motionless, except for the tiniest quiver in the curve of her lip, and it broke my heart.

"Come on," I said, holding out a hand toward her. "We can walk from here."

3

SHELTER

Emily didn't take my hand, but she did move to walk beside me. I wasn't sure it would have worked out that way if not for the mention of her sister. She had to be starving, so when we crossed in front of a shop that was actually open, I deposited her between two brick columns beside the storefront window.

"Stay here, I'll be right back."

She glanced up at the sign hanging above us before giving me a raised brow. It read something like "tobacco," "spirits," and "open all nite," in heavy script. I didn't attempt an explanation.

This wasn't the busiest part of town and I knew pickings would be slim, but that didn't stop me from grimacing at the selection of foodstuffs inside what had to be the dirtiest display case I'd ever laid eyes on. I took the last two plastic-wrapped packages that I assumed were sub sandwiches and three bottles of water to the counter, where I added a handful of jerky sticks from a wire display rack and took one deep breath before looking up.

The cashier was old in a way only a hard life can make a person. His grayed hair stood in thin tufts that were likely once curls. His skin fell slack and wrinkled over hollow cheeks, and his eyes were downcast and uninterested in me. I reached forward, as if sliding my merchandise closer, and then grasped the ashen skin of his mottled hand. His eyes shot to mine and I prayed the gift hadn't left me.

I didn't like to steal. I earned my living where I could. Where the Council had let me. But right at this moment, I didn't have much choice. I stared into his eyes and focused my energy on hypnotizing him with both sight and touch. His pupils flinched an instant before his face relaxed, and I tried not to lose myself in the relief that it had worked.

Two minutes later, I was back in the street with Emily, who examined the shape of my brown paper sack. Apparently satisfied it couldn't possibly be a bottle of liquor, she followed me the three more blocks we had to walk for what passed as a hotel.

Like the package store, the hotel didn't list a name on the exterior of the building. Flecks of faded white paint had long since been swept away, leaving the word "rooms" checked with the red brick beneath it. I glanced sidelong at Emily, expecting at least some sign of protest, but she seemed beyond that now. She waited by the entrance while I acquired a key, and then trailed numbly behind as we climbed the seven flights of stairs to the room. When we finally made it inside, she fell into a chair without so much as a glance at the questionable stains marking the cushion.

If I had been a psychopathic killer, her mood would have taken the fun right out of it.

I secured the door and briefly glanced out the window to assure myself of an escape route before I joined her. I resisted the urge to apologize as I sat two bottles of water on her side of the small round table between smashed gray-brown globs of hardened chewing gum.

"Drink," I said, and she straightened a bit as she came out of her trance to take a bottle.

When she'd finished about half without heaving or any of the other terrible scenarios I'd formed in my head, I unwrapped the first sandwich and surreptitiously sniffed for signs of rot. I was fairly certain it was ham, and there didn't appear to be much for toppings, which made me feel moderately better about handing it over. Emily took the offering without question and I sat my own sandwich and water on my side of the table before dumping the remaining contents in the center. The three jerky sticks didn't look out of place in our sad little situation.

The pain in my shoulder had dulled, but I knew it

wouldn't fully heal until I'd slept, and that was the last thing I could do here.

I became aware of Emily's stillness and glanced over to find her watching me, half-eaten sandwich rewrapped and lying on the table. She was clearly exhausted and probably traumatized, but alive.

I'd saved her.

After a moment, I said, "Aern."

"Huh?"

"It's Aern," I explained. "My name."

She nodded, unsure how to respond. I wondered if she was in shock, or still convinced I was a crazy person.

"You're shivering," I said, and then stood, thinking what a stupid remark it had been as I pulled the threadbare blanket from the bed.

"I dropped my jacket," she mumbled through trembling lips.

By the time she wrapped herself in the blanket, she'd progressed to shuddering. I forced myself to let her. To not touch her.

I sat again in the chair across from her, and the room was quiet for a long while. When she at last broke the silence, I was lost in thought and her soft voice sounded too loud.

"It wasn't my car."

I gave her a questioning look and she went on.

"The car, the one I used to follow you, it wasn't mine. I... I stole it from my foster parent."

I realized my face betrayed my surprise, but I couldn't do much for it.

"That's the good news, right? It didn't have my name on it, just his and an old address. And even if they find him"—she shifted under her cover—"well, he's a bastard."

Her eyes met mine in a challenge, but relaxed when she didn't find the answering one in my expression. In fact, I'd schooled my features to blank attentiveness, though I was severely concerned about both her comment and where this discussion was headed. *Don't ask*, I thought. *Leave it be. We've got bigger problems right now.*

And whatever he'd done to earn the label, Emily was right, they *would* find him.

"The bad news?" I asked evenly.

"Yeah," she said. "That would be my bag."

A memory of the lumpy duffle bag flashed in my mind, along with a dozen or so ideas of what it could have held. School books? Gym clothes? Chinese throwing stars?

She sighed. "Things have been kind of rough for me and Bri." She winced at her own use of the name and my gut twisted. "I try to keep us together, to make things work." She shook her head. "That doesn't matter. The thing is, the bad news"—her eyes came back to mine—"everything important was in that bag. Everything I'd need. To run."

It took immeasurable strength not to respond to her words, not to allow myself to envision what they'd been going through, what had happened to her and to Brianna.

I forced myself to remain composed, voice steady. "Can you tell me what, exactly?"

"There were a few things"—she hesitated, looked away—"from my mother."

"What about your sister, Emily? Was there anything in that bag that linked you to her?"

A sick horror crossed her face. "Why? What... do you mean they'll go after her?"

"No. No, I told you she was safe."

Emily was bolt upright now, her blanket gathered in her lap as if she meant to run for Brianna that very instant. To save her.

I reached across the table to stop her, but dropped my hand before it got halfway. "They can't get to her now," I explained. "They don't know where she's at."

She relaxed a fraction. "Then why? What are you asking me?"

I sighed. "They'll come after you. To use you against her."

Her face went pale. "There's a photo of us. And some paperwork. It won't be a question."

Her words hung between us for a long while as she waited for me to reply, to tell her everything would be okay, but I couldn't.

"What will they do?" she finally asked.

I shook my head. "It doesn't matter."

Emily was suddenly standing. "How will they use me against her? What will they do?"

Once more, I resisted the impulse to reach out to her. Instead, I gave her what truth I could. "They would... use you. To draw her out."

Emily seemed to deflate as the vehemence left her. She'd seen me strung up, no doubt seen the blade threatening me. She was smart enough to imagine what their "use" of her would entail. She'd be wrong, though. The Council—Morgan—they would do much, much worse.

But she could imagine.

"It doesn't matter," I repeated. "They won't get to you. And Brianna is safe." I gestured toward the bed. "You should get some sleep, we shouldn't stay here too long."

She stared at me for two full minutes before finally glancing at the bed. I had no idea what was going through her mind, but it wasn't the need for rest. She sat again in the chair and pulled the thin, faded-blue blanket tight against her cheeks. The bottom half of her face was buried as she simply stared across the otherwise empty room toward the only door.

In hopes that she would eventually give in, I clicked the lamp off, leaving the room with only the dim light filtering through the curtains, and then spun the very uncomfortable chair in which I sat around, kicked my feet up on the bedside table, and tilted my head back against my laced fingers. I closed my eyes to the stained plaster ceiling, but I had no intention of sleeping. Emily needed to rest. We would be running again in the morning, and whether Morgan's men found us or not, it wasn't going to be easy.

It was more than an hour later when she spoke again, this time her words barely above a whisper.

"I know you didn't kidnap her."

When I didn't reply, she went on.

"I saw her leave with you. I just… I just couldn't believe she would go like that, that she would leave without saying anything…"

Emily was struggling, and I didn't need her admission, but I let her go on. Because she needed it.

"I knew something was wrong," she said, "I couldn't get her to tell me. She was always like that, though. Always keeping things from me, so I wouldn't get upset. Always pretending everything was fine. But she just left…"

She was questioning now, and I could give her that answer at least. "She wanted to keep you safe."

Her low voice came tremulous now from the darkness. "From who?"

"Morgan," I said.

She repeated the name, as if committing it to memory.

"He wants your sister."

There was a long silence as she built up the courage to ask, "For what?"

I sighed. "You won't believe me. It's more of that crazy person stuff."

She didn't question me again, didn't demand that I tell her, didn't try to convince me she would believe, and I felt oddly that she'd accepted that answer. Accepted it much too easily.

And then I wondered instead if she was just imagining what crazy people did with their hostages.

"He won't hurt her," I said. "I promise you that. He needs her alive."

Emily swallowed hard, but she didn't sob.

The room fell silent again and eventually, after a very long while, her breathing became even and subdued.

I finally relaxed. It was the first time in days.

4

HEIGHTS

Sunrise was still hours away when the metallic tick of a key meeting the lock echoed across the room. I leapt to my feet; we had only seconds before they would see us. I reached for Emily, meaning to cover her mouth and sweep her from the chair, but she was already standing, apparently too on edge for real sleep. Her eyes were wide in the darkness and I was struck again by the resemblance to her sister.

The key turned and I grabbed Emily's wrist. I'd secured the door, but they would see in soon enough, and I didn't want them to know how close they'd gotten.

I slipped through the window first, perching awkwardly on the thin metal framework that surrounded it as I pulled

Emily through behind me. She automatically began to climb down, but I stopped her. She glanced at my grip on her arm and then back at me questioningly. I shook my head and pointed up. It was hard to tell in the dim light of the distant street lamps, but I was pretty sure her face went pale.

I stood, releasing her arm to climb higher, and trusted that she would follow. Paint cracked beneath my fingers on the wrought iron, flaking down to the alley below. Seven flights. Eight. I looked back for Emily.

Her hands were shaking as she reached above her head for another piece of railing. She froze when the solid thud of someone shouldering into an old wood door sounded below. In our room.

"Faster," I whispered, wincing at the pain as I reached again for the balustrade overhead. We had three more stories before they were to the window. And only moments after that before they realized we weren't on the street below. If we could make it, we'd be safe.

A quiet gasp and the squeak of rubber against metal seemed to fracture the air and I pushed away from the wall to see Emily hanging by a tenuous handhold while her feet dangled beneath her. I started to shuffle back down but she regained her footing and pulled herself once more to the relative safety of the railing.

I watched her climb until she was only two flights from the roof.

The railing didn't reach far enough, so I clung to the block where I could find dips, edges, anything to grip, but I was barely able to secure my footing. The last few feet were a credit to the soles of my shoes and sheer luck, and I knew Emily wouldn't be able to follow on her own. As soon as I had hold of the ledge, I looked for her, and for the window below.

Emily was a flight down, still climbing.

A dark shape leaned from the window of our room.

I pulled myself up silently, and immediately hooked my foot behind a roof vent to lean back over the ledge. Emily was frantically searching the wall for her next handhold and I reached out, motioning for her to take my hand. Her expression went incredulous for one moment, and then, as if remembering why we were scaling a twelve-story building, she looked for the window below.

Her chest was heaving when she looked up at me again. I couldn't say that I blamed her. She was eleven and half stories up, barely hanging on by less than sturdy decorative railings, and the man below us wanted to kill her. I wished I could say her name. Distract her. Something. But all I could do was offer my hand, tell her with my eyes it would be okay.

She stared at my outstretched hand, completely immobilized with fear. Her knuckles were white, and no doubt her bloodless fingers would give in soon. Her eyes moved to meet mine, and I could see the reluctant reasoning she was doing in her stare.

She would have to trust me.

Below her, the man looked up. I didn't move my gaze from Emily's, only held my hand steady, willing her to take it.

The man climbed onto the ledge outside our window and the old wrought iron creaked. A silent gasp registered on Emily's face, but I couldn't stop her from looking down.

"*Emily.*" My whisper was harsh, demanding, and fell upon deaf ears.

The man reached for the balustrade above his head, and began to heft himself toward us.

I repeated her name, this time above a whisper. I didn't suppose it mattered now.

Emily looked back to me, and it was as if all the emotion I'd expected from her through our entire ordeal, all of the natural responses I'd been denied, hit her in that one moment.

"Take my hand," I said levelly.

She swallowed hard. Her eyes stayed on me as she concentrated on uncurling her fingers from the grip she had on the railing. The metal below creaked in a way it had not with our weight as the man progressed upward. I nodded as Emily forced one finger at a time free from their fossilized positions.

When she finally reached a trembling hand for mine, my chest began to unknot. I almost had her. We would make it. All that was left was to get her within my grip, pull her to the roof, and…

The creak of metal was different this time, somehow final. It cut through my thoughts just before it erupted into more: a metallic groan and crack, then clinks, then the heavy thud of weighted flesh slamming repeatedly against rail and block and...

"No." I tried to hold Emily's gaze, tried to force her to stay with me instead of looking down, to reach those few extra inches and take my hand. But she didn't.

It was poor timing to say the least. A sickening, wet thwump was followed by only the echo of clanging metal as the piece that gave landed beside the broken body on the alley floor, and then bounced a few times before settling to its own death.

"Emily," I repeated, surprised that my tone so resembled begging, "please."

She was panting now, a kind of noiseless, heaving panic taken over when she looked back to me. But that didn't scare me as much as the tears.

"Take my hand," I said. "Take my hand and it will all be okay."

Her face twisted in disbelief, horror. How could it ever be okay?

"You'll be safe. Just take my hand and you will be safe."

Don't think about the bloody bits of man below you. Don't think about it. Take my hand.

She reached for me again, and I wondered if my sway had finally worked, if I'd finally gotten through to her. Her palm was slick with sweat, but I'd have to do with the grip I had. There was no way I could trust my other shoulder, my recently broken shoulder, to pull her up.

We stared at each other for a long moment while she convinced herself to let go with her other hand.

"I've got you, Emily." I nodded. "Let go, use your feet against the building and grab hold of my arm."

Her eyes closed in one long blink, and when she opened them, the rest of her weight pulled against our connected hands. Her other palm smacked against my forearm and clung an instant before her right sneaker slipped from its brace on the bricks. As she dangled there, the terror in her expression was suddenly gone, and determination took its place.

She found her footing again, gritted her teeth, and pushed upward as I pulled, both of us struggling to bring her to the safety of the roof. There was a fleeting moment of mindless scrabbling at the ledge, and then she was over, rushing forward as I got to my feet, and I dragged her away from the edge and into my arms out of reflex, pulling her body close to mine.

I'd like to think she shared in the instant of joy and utter relief, but after some brief, unnamed time, I suddenly realized her body had gone rigid. And that I was hugging her.

I slowly relaxed my arms and stepped back. "I... I'm sorry." Why was I apologizing?

Emily stared blankly at me and I wanted badly for her to say something. Anything.

"Emily..."

She went pale and leaned forward as if to heave, started toward the ledge with that intent, and then appeared to remember what was below.

She swallowed hard, and I fought the urge not to laugh in a strange surge of hysteria. She would just not be sick, then. I shook my head. My chest finally allowed me a full, deep breath, and I took it gratefully.

Given that our pursuer lay smashed at the bottom of the building, we weren't in such a dire hurry as we had been. But I had no desire to be on the rooftop when the police showed up, if anyone had actually noticed the commotion. As soon as Emily had gathered herself enough to move, I helped her cross to the empty building three rooftops over.

There were no real gaps between the buildings, so it wasn't as if she had to leap across, but Emily couldn't stop glancing nervously down.

"Do you need to rest for a minute?" I asked as we approached the structure that housed the access door on the last roof.

She shook her head. "Just get me down."

I tried not to smile. "You're all right now. We'll get out of here and find a new place to stay until morning."

She didn't reply, only stayed on my heels with her head down, so I kept talking.

"This is an old office building. It was closed years ago, no one will be in it."

I picked up a discarded piece of metal to pry the lock before I realized it had already been busted, and hoped I was right about the building being empty.

"There is access to the parking garage on the second

floor, and then we'll just slip out and take a quick run to somewhere new." *Somewhere no people are, no one Morgan can direct*, I thought as I drew open the door.

She followed me wordlessly as I grabbed a flashlight and a few tools from the maintenance area beside the access door, and then quickly located the stairwell. When we reached the second floor, I stopped to let her rest, but she didn't appear to need it as much as I had expected. She must have been on the track team, or maybe a marathoner, because the last few days were beginning to wear on even me.

We moved from the stairwell across the vacant office, which was only discernible from the carpet discoloration in the shape of cubicle walls, and found the hallway that led to the garage entrance.

"Hold this," I said, handing Emily the flashlight.

She held it steady, but stepped back when I took a screwdriver much like the one she'd nearly killed me with from my pocket. I worked the locks loose and pried the door open far enough to bust the catch free, and then tossed the tools to the ground once we were through. They clattered, and it echoed with our footfalls across the dark, empty parking garage as we ran through the concrete expanse.

Fortunately, the first level was partially underground, so the leap needed to reach the ground was not deadly. However, you couldn't have told Emily that.

"No," she said, staring down at what was once a patch of manicured lawn between two concrete curbs.

"What?" I glanced right and left, nearly certain no one was in the shadows.

She stepped back from the ledge. "Let's just use the door."

"We can't, the lock there is—" I stared at her. "Are you afraid of heights?"

The dim light from outside hid her face where she stood, so I moved the flashlight to see her. The blush of embarrassment her cheeks held turned immediately to a flush of anger. "No."

I glanced back down to hide my grin. It really wasn't that far, but the shadows probably made it seem twice as bad to her eyes. I'd have to lead her across the ledge to the lowest slant and we could jump from there. If she admitted it, the whole thing would be easier on both of us. Besides, she'd just scaled a twelve-story building.

"I don't see the problem," I said.

She huffed. Crossed her arms. "I'm not doing it. It's stupid."

I held the flashlight again to her face and shrugged. "There's no other way. If you're afraid—"

She suddenly came at me, or at least that was what I thought was happening, and I jumped back. But she shoved past me and climbed onto the concrete half wall surrounding the garage.

"Emily, wait."

But it was too late, I was talking to air. I stared blankly into the night for a moment, and then sighed. This girl was so not Brianna.

5

ZOMBIES

I supposed being angry with me was better than mulling over what had just happened, so I let Emily march ahead of me for the first two blocks of our escape. The silent treatment had its advantages as well, because I needed to be positive no one had followed us this time.

Probably the hotel clerk had given us away the last time, because it would have been unusual for a teenage girl and a rakish twenty-two-year-old to be checking in to that particular establishment at that particular hour. The corner of my mouth lifted at the description in my head and Emily gave me her best evil-eye glare when she spotted it.

I cleared my throat. "The sun's coming up, so traffic will

pick up soon. We should probably jog from here. It's not more than a few blocks, are you up for it?"

Her mouth pressed together, holding in a retort I thought, and she nodded.

We kept an easy pace, and I got the feeling the task made Emily feel better. At the very least, she wouldn't be missing her coat. It was actually more like six blocks to the residential area, and another four to the empty houses. I slowed to walk the last block, casually taking a blacktop drive to the back yard of one of the houses, in the unlikely case that someone was around to see us. From there, we cut through two more yards for a house that I was confident could keep us safe for at least a few hours' rest.

I slid a hand over the trim of the door, then turned a few rocks in the landscaping beside the back step before I found a key.

"Is this your house?" Emily whispered from behind me. "Because that would be a really dumb place to hide."

I nearly laughed. "No. We're just using it for a bit. No one lives here." I slid the key into the lock. "It's for sale, but no one's buying." I glanced back at her. "We don't have to worry about the real estate agent dropping by. They probably wish the whole lot would burn."

She only hesitated a moment before she walked in. To a dark house. With a stranger. I sighed again, and then tossed the key onto the counter before locking the door behind us.

This particular house was not entirely empty. Short, orange

patterned curtains hung above the kitchen windows, and the previous owner had left a few items they hadn't considered worth packing when they moved. A yellowed clock over the stove proclaimed home was where the hearth was, its hour hand permanently stuck on two, minute hand dangling loosely toward six. A stack of newspapers rested on a corner shelf, a half-empty bottle of dish detergent by the sink.

Emily stood in the center of the room, somehow appropriate with her baggy gray shirt and loose, tangled hair. Her jeans bore the scuffs and dirt of old brick and roof tar, and she was pale, and tired, and sad.

And I was staring at her.

I jerked back to life. "There's no power, and you should stay away from the front windows, but we're good here." I gestured toward the hall. "I'll check the basement for supplies, you can find a place to sleep, the restroom."

She nodded.

We stood there for a moment, as I couldn't seem to find the will to leave. When it finally became awkward, Emily turned to go.

"If you need me," I said to her back, "yell."

She'd paused when I started speaking, and she only nodded in acknowledgement, but her shoulders lifted the slightest bit as she carried herself from the room.

The basement was damp, dark, and littered with empty food jars and butter tubs. I was able to find two jugs of distilled water, though only one was sealed, and an old moving blanket on the shelves near the water heater. I slid the flashlight I'd taken from the office building into the back pocket of my jeans and took the steps two at a time, water in one hand, blanket in the other.

I hadn't realized how fast I was moving until I saw Emily through a door in the hall and had to take three backward steps to see her again.

She was standing in front of a mirrored vanity in the center of a small washroom, pulling her hair back with a tie she'd apparently found in one of the drawers, all of which now stood open from her rummaging. The sun was coming in through a high window to silhouette the line of her neck, her bare arms. I wasn't certain if the sight was a shock because her baggy clothes had been so misleading, or if I'd just not had a free moment to fully appreciate her, but I was suddenly transfixed as she secured the band, and then dropped her hands, ponytail falling into place, and looked at me.

I swallowed. Mentally shook myself. Held up the hand with the water jugs.

I explained she should drink from the sealed container and wash with the other, but I had the feeling she was used to making do with what she could find. She hadn't apparently had any issue with ransacking the cabinets.

I held up the blanket and pointed down the hall. "I'll find you a place to rest."

She nodded, but she was concentrating mostly on opening the drinking water.

The last two rooms down the hall were empty, so I chose the one with carpet, and windows facing away from the light. In the unlikely event we'd be found, we should be able make it across the hall to the alternate escape route. The carpet was pile and would be more comfortable than the hardwood in the opposite room. Warmer, too. Emily must be freezing without a coat. And I'd have to do something for food. This place was pretty miserable as far as shelters went.

"I don't really care," Emily said from behind me.

"What?"

"That stain you're staring at, I don't really care what it is." She took the blanket as she walked past me. "As long as I can sit down, it can stay there and be as nasty as it wants."

"I was thinking about food," I said. "I'll need to get you something to eat."

She glanced out the window, and then back at me to shrug. "I'm fine for a while."

With a long breath, she slid her back down the wall beside the window to sit and unfolded the blanket. I walked to the casement and twisted the vinyl blinds shut. They were a poor fit, probably a temporary solution by the realtor.

When I turned, Emily was holding one end of the blanket out for me.

I didn't move quickly enough. She said, "It's cold."

I nodded. "I'll find you a coat as well." I stepped around her to sit on her other side, leaving a careful eight inches between us.

Overnight, the temperatures had dipped. We'd be more comfortable traveling during the day, but we'd also be more apt to be spotted. I'd have to get her to a safe house. And since Morgan knew who she was, I couldn't get her there soon enough.

"Aern?"

Emily's voice, so close and speaking my name, sent a very peculiar feeling through me.

I went completely still and then, quite unintentionally, moved toward her when I turned my head to answer. "Yes?"

It was the closest I'd been to her when she wasn't trying to kill me.

"How did you know about this place? About how to find your way in the office building?"

And it was answer time. I resisted the urge to cringe. "I'd been watching Morgan's men. Misleading them."

She stared at me. I was explaining poorly, expecting her to make terrible leaps in my logic. I tried again. "Some of Morgan's men have been working out of the area near the warehouse. I've been trying to keep an eye on them, and trying to keep them away from Brianna."

I could see a protest form immediately on Emily's lips and held up a hand. "Bri is safe. I promise. They have no way of finding her. But if they see me on the run, they're going to assume I'm working alone, and that I have her."

Emily straightened to face me, her shoulder braced against the wall. "You don't have her?"

"I can't tell you where she is, Emily. It's the only thing keeping her safe. If they find you—"

She cut me off. "You think I would tell them where she is?"

"I think you would rather die first." I purposefully lowered the tone of my own voice to keep her anger in check. "But they wouldn't need to ask. You could do nothing but tell them."

Emily didn't ask why. Instead, she said, "Those men, the two who were chasing us."

I nodded.

"Those were Morgan's men?"

"Yes." I shook my head. "No. They weren't…" I sighed. "Emily, I have to tell you something you're probably not going to believe."

The corner of her mouth pulled down in a grimace. "Go for it."

"Those men weren't like Morgan. The man in the car and the man in the hotel were only commonbloods."

Emily looked a little sick. I hoped it was only the thought of their smashed bodies.

"They were merely men in the wrong place at the wrong time. And Morgan used them. Like throwaways."

"How… what do you mean?"

"They were under his control. It's like a trance, and they have to do what he wants."

She didn't even flinch. "They drove into a brick wall and climbed a building."

"Anything," I repeated. "Whatever he wants them to do."

"He didn't want them to die," she said numbly.

"No, their goal was to get to us. Death was an unfortunate accident."

She shifted slightly, reflecting on what I'd said. "Like a trance?"

"We call it sway."

"And he can do it to anyone?"

I cautiously formed my answer. "All commonbloods can be swayed."

Her eyes shifted to mine again, and then went slightly unfocused. She was silent for several minutes.

She said, "So they're like zombies. Brainless zombies coming to kill us."

Her description had me taken aback for moment, but I finally answered, leaving out that at the moment they only wanted to kill her, not me. "No. Definitely not brainless. They're just under sway, under a direction they can't stop heading toward until they've completed it. Their brains still function otherwise, they can use everything they already know to reach his goal."

"Smart zombies," she said.

I smiled wryly, conceded.

"And this Morgan, he can turn anyone with his sway, make them do what he wants." She bit her lip. "An endless supply of smart zombies."

The smile fell from my face.

"Well, I suppose it's good to know what we're up against," she said.

I stared at her.

She nodded. "Yeah, well, my sister always makes me find the positive in any situation."

She moved back against the wall and leaned her head and shoulder against me.

"And you called her Bri," she murmured.

6

PROPHECY

For the first five minutes, I couldn't believe she was lying against me. And then I recalled the ache in my injured shoulder. Where she lay. I was fairly certain she'd fallen right to sleep, but I still didn't move for another half hour.

When I finally shifted, my arm gave a scream of relief and my shoulder a cry of pain. Emily mumbled something unintelligible and slid lower until her head rested on my leg and her shoulder against the floor. I attempted to adjust the blanket to better cover her, but she had it tucked up under her chin in a tight fist.

And then my arm just hovered there, over her. She was finally still. And cold. And had lost her sister.

Everything about her begged to be touched. And yet, even with her head against my leg, I hesitated. It seemed important somehow. My hand ached to wrap around her. I settled for an elbow, placing the length of my arm over hers to keep her warm, and she squeezed her arms tighter into her chest, and then snuggled closer.

It was becoming harder not to fall asleep. After so many hours, my breath began to match the slow, drawn-out rhythm of hers. Our body heat began to level out between the cover and carpet, and even the ache of my shoulder became a dull background noise to the dust motes that danced in the tiny rays of dim light filtering through the blinds. My eyelids were getting heavy, but I knew I couldn't sleep. Not even here.

There was no way to be certain Morgan couldn't find us. No guarantee that at any moment a dark figure wouldn't pass in front of our window on its way to the door, leaving no more than a brief shadow in its wake... a brief shadow over the dust motes floating among the rays of afternoon light.

I cursed, suddenly roused from my stupor.

Emily jerked awake. I held her still for a moment, my hand hard on her shoulder. I didn't hear the door.

I slid carefully from beneath her, and then tight against the wall to see out the window. A tall, dark-skinned man in a business suit was crossing the lawn. He peered into the windows of the house next door, and then crossed the street to check there.

I watched him until he was three houses down. Emily moved silently beside me, her body flat against the wall in waiting.

"He's looking for us," I whispered, "but it seems pretty random. He's undoubtedly swept the entire area."

Emily leaned in front of me to peek out the space between the blind and the frame.

Her face was inches from mine when she whispered hopefully, "He left his car."

I shook my head. "Right now, they don't know we're here. If we take the car, we'd be giving them a lead."

She nodded, and the little sigh of breath she let go hit the skin of my neck.

I had to touch her again. My hand found her waist. "We need to let him get out of here, report back that he didn't find any sign of us. And then we'll go."

"To Brianna?" she asked.

"To a safe house. Somewhere Morgan can't find you and the others can protect you." And I would have to leave her.

"Is that where Bri is?" she said. "I know you can't tell me, but I mean, is that the kind of place she's in?"

Against all reason, my head gave a small nod.

"Then why can't we go there?" She leaned closer, her whispers taking on an edge of desperation. "If she's safe there, then we'd be safe there."

"No. I won't risk it. Morgan is searching for us as we speak."

"He's searching for her, too," she argued. "And if all he plans to do with me is use me against Brianna, then the best place for us to be is together. If he gets to her, then at least I'll be with her."

"I can't take you to her."

"But—"

I cut her off. "I will keep her from Morgan. I won't risk him getting to her. There are things you don't know, and you're just going to have to trust me until I sort things out."

She opened her mouth to protest and then suddenly stopped. I couldn't tell whether she'd held back her retort, or simply realized she was nearly pressed up against me as we argued in undertones. She stepped back and leaned once more on the wall, staring across the room rapt in thought.

We were both silent as the man reappeared on the street and walked toward his car. The muffled thump of a car door, and then the engine turning over, and he was driving away. And I was alone with Emily again, with seventy miles of road between us and the safe house I wanted her in.

When dusk settled, I returned the blanket and now empty water jugs to the basement, and restored the key to its place beneath a landscaping rock. We walked through several backyards until we were forced to go street side. The first occupied house we came to had a boarded-up front window and a rust-orange clunker in the driveway that didn't look as if it was likely to start.

We kept on a few more blocks, though I didn't want to

go too far, because every home we passed was a gamble of being spotted. Remembered. When we finally came to a nicer block house with a promising sedan in the drive, I pressed Emily to hide by the garage.

"If Morgan's men come here, they'll be more likely to ask whether the two of us were seen."

She went along with the plan, but I didn't think she trusted it.

I knocked on the door, a deep evergreen with white trim, and waited. A gold-plated mailbox hung loose on the red brick, its hinged door stuck partially open. Faded lava rock filled the otherwise empty flower beds. I could see the scuffed white toe of one of Emily's sneakers peeking out from the corner of the house. Maybe she was scared. Or planned on listening…

"Yeah?" the old man croaked when he opened the door. He wore a robe over a stained white tank top and belted slacks.

I stared into his smoky gray eyes. "Ask me to come in," I urged in a tone low enough not to carry.

He stared blankly for a moment, and then stepped back. "Come in, young man. Come in."

Fifteen minutes later, Emily and I were driving a 1992 Pontiac down Emerson toward the freeway.

She spoke around a mouthful of ham sandwich. "You didn't kill him or something, did you?"

I laughed.

She swallowed her bite. "I'm serious."

"You decided to eat his food before you asked?"

She took a long swig of water. "No. I just didn't think of it until then."

"I've never killed anyone, for a Pontiac or no."

"Good," she said. "He isn't hurt?"

I glanced at her. She meant it. "He isn't hurt, I swear it."

And, once again, she didn't ask what he *was*.

The old man didn't have much, but at least I'd been able to get us a car with half a tank of gas and something to eat. I'd used my sway to convince him he'd not seen us, but if Morgan did the asking himself, it wouldn't stick.

"Aern?" Emily put down the empty napkin that had held her sandwich.

"Yes?"

"What about the others? The ones you said would protect me."

"I don't want to tell you that," I said.

"Because it isn't safe for me to know? Because he can get information from me?"

I thought, *Because I'm not sure myself*. I said, "It's better this way. I wouldn't keep it from you if I didn't have good reason."

"Okay," she murmured. She was thoughtful for a moment. "And you have good reason to trust them with me?"

She was asking all the wrong questions. I pursed my lips. "They will keep Brianna from Morgan at all costs, Emily."

And again, she simply nodded. Not asking why her sister

was in the middle of a fight between Morgan and some untold others. Not asking why this one girl was so important.

I pulled the car to the side of the road and stared at her.

"Emily, is there something you're not telling me?"

She froze mid-bite of her second sandwich. Her face went pale. I waited.

"Wh—" She lowered the sandwich. "What do you mean?"

I took one calming breath. "I mean you're taking this whole thing very well. I mean I'm risking everything to keep your sister safe. I mean, so help me, if you're sitting on something—"

Her face went hard and she leaned forward. "Don't you threaten me, you... you..." She stopped and went for a new tactic. "Listen, no one asked you to save Brianna. We. Were. Fine. You didn't have to come along and steal her from me for some sick—"

"Sick what?"

"I don't know, okay. I don't have any idea."

I narrowed my eyes on her and her shoulders fell in defeat. She tossed the sandwich in the bag and slapped her hands against her thighs in frustration.

"Maybe I don't want to tell you, either."

"Fine," I said. "But if you're keeping something from me that will endanger Brianna—"

She huffed indignantly. "I would *never* risk Bri." Her hands came up to cover her face and she took several long breaths. She mumbled something incoherent.

I pulled her hands down. "I can't understand what you're saying."

She stared at me for a moment. "I can't tell you," she said quietly. "I don't think I can tell anyone."

My mouth went dry. I realized her hands were still in mine, and I drew mine back to the steering wheel.

"It's not... Aern, it's not that I don't trust you. I can see that you're helping. It's just..." Her eyes flicked down and then back to me. "It's just that my whole life, it's been our secret, mine and Brianna's."

"So this is something Brianna knows?" I felt suddenly more at ease. Brianna knew Morgan was after her, she would have told us if it was imperative to stopping him.

Emily bit her lip.

I mentally cursed. "Emily, if it's important..."

"I would never do anything to hurt my sister," she said. "I would never keep anything from her that wasn't... that I didn't have to."

So Brianna didn't know. "I can't be swayed, Emily. Nothing you tell me can be ripped from my mind, do you understand that?"

"I think I do," she whispered. A hand came up to rub her temple, and suddenly, she wasn't speaking to me. "I never thought this would happen. It was all too crazy."

"It doesn't have to happen," I said. "We can stop it."

She stared at her hands in her lap for a long moment. When she finally spoke again, her fingers twisted together. "I never believed her. How could I? It was ridiculous, a story." She rubbed her palms against her legs. "I didn't tell Brianna. I just couldn't. At first, it was because I thought she was fibbing." She shook her head and glanced up at me with an embarrassed smile. "That's what she called it, fibbing."

Emily's eyes were so sad, I couldn't bring myself to smile back, only nod.

"She was always a little eccentric, odd. She didn't like us to go out in public, always wanted us right there with her. She told us wild fairy tales as if they were true. But this, this one was different. And it was only for me." She drew a shaky breath. "That's what she said. Only for me. I was never to tell Brianna."

"Your mother?" I asked.

She nodded. "I didn't know. Until she died, I never believed." She waved her hand. "Then they shipped us off to foster homes and it was a constant struggle to stay together. How could I tell her then? How could I tell Brianna she just lost her mother because..."

"Because of the prophecy."

"It's my job to protect her," she said. "I'm the only one who can keep her safe."

So she knew. All along, she'd known. But she was wrong, she wasn't the one to save Brianna. "The prophecy never mentioned twins, Emily. There's no reference to you at all. I understand how you feel, but you weren't meant to take this on yourself. Your mother should have never put that on you."

Her eyes were hard on mine. "She wasn't wrong about the rest of it."

She had me there, things weren't exactly going as planned on either side. "Maybe so," I said. "But you aren't the only one trying to save Brianna."

Emily's eyes softened and she nodded. And then she brought her legs up to her chest and hugged her knees to look out the passenger window, effectively ending the conversation.

7

CHANGE OF PLANS

I'd already told her too much. Emily was no minor player, she wasn't simply a victim unwittingly caught up in her sister's mess. There was no safe house in existence that could hold her. She was determined to save her sister, and, one way or another, she'd unquestionably end up in the middle of it all.

And just because I couldn't seem to get her to do what I wanted didn't mean Morgan wouldn't.

I was going to have to do something different, and I didn't like having to change my plans. Annoyed, I took my eyes from the road to glance over at her where she leaned against the window, knees pulled up and thumb wrapped inside the seatbelt at her shoulder. She was staring out into the night, and the tiny strands of hair that had pulled loose from her ponytail caught the light of the oncoming car.

Had I not been staring at her, I would have missed the truck that was passing that car, lights off and heading straight for Emily.

She screamed.

I swerved and ran the car up over the curb, but wasn't able to avoid impact. The truck slammed the rear quarter of the car, spinning us around in the intersection, where another car smashed into the front panel on my side. We were pinned, but still moving. Tearing metal screeched through the car and Emily's wide eyes found me as she searched for escape. I released the buckle on her safety belt and tried to push my door open. It was stuck, jammed from the collision with the other car which, judging from the horrified look on the driver's face, must have been involved only by chance.

The window was jammed as well, so I turned to climb over the back seat and saw Emily grasping for the handle on her side.

"No!" I yelled.

Her head whipped around to first find me, and then, realizing why I'd stopped her, the truck that was even now pushing against the back of our car.

I was over the seat in a heartbeat and dragged Emily behind me. The only warning I gave her before opening the door was, "Run. Don't stop, don't look behind you."

I had her arm and was towing her for the first few steps, but once we hit sidewalk, she was running. I could hear the engine of the truck revving behind us, but it was trapped in the chaos of a six-car pile-up, and had to plow through several stopped vehicles to reach us. It did just that.

"Turn," I yelled, and Emily listened, heading straight down the first side street. Two more blocks, and we'd have been on the interstate. They should have let us. It would have worked.

"Right," I said at the next block. We'd gotten lucky. We had a chance. But how had he found us?

"Aern," Emily called from beside me, "you're bleeding."

I pressed Emily closer to the buildings as we ran, dodging an elderly couple with a pushcart. When I glanced down, I saw the long gash on my arm from the twisted metal of the car. "I'm fine," I said. "Are you all right?"

She laughed breathlessly as we sprinted down another block and turned left.

When we finally stopped running, the whirr of emergency sirens was only a distant hum. Emily leaned against the back entrance of a Chinese restaurant, gasping for breath while I decided what to do first.

"I need to make a call," I said.

Emily nodded and pushed against the wall to standing.

The door banged open and I shoved her back, pressing my own body alongside hers as a dishwasher slung a bin of food scrap into the trash. He spared us no more than a disapproving head shake as he turned and spotted us, a couple of delinquents making out in the alley, so I grabbed the door right before it slammed behind him.

"What are you doing?" Emily hissed.

"I'll be right back," I said. "Don't move."

I peeked in to find a short hall that split toward the kitchen and two alcoves. The one to the right, the only one I could see into from my vantage point, held the alarm system and electrical box. I was hoping the one on the left had what we needed.

Through the steam of stir-fry, I watched the cooks and staff for a pattern. Seeing there was none, I took a chance and slipped inside the door and around the corner.

Jackpot.

I found two jackets, a ball cap, and the cell phone before I threw a few more items on the haul for good measure. When I peered around the corner to check the coast, it was all clear. The sizzle and clatter of the kitchen didn't falter so I didn't expect anyone to follow us, but I didn't test our luck. When I shoved the door open, Emily lurched back, having been standing right next to it, and I grabbed her arm to run with me to the end of the alley and behind another dumpster.

"What—" She stopped mid-sentence to examine the jacket I shoved at her. "You're kidding," she said.

I smiled. "It'll look good on you. Besides, I didn't have time to be picky."

Her eyes narrowed on me, but she slid her arms into the gold silk sleeves.

I shrugged on a dark twill jacket and pulled the baseball cap low on my head. It only made things worse.

"This is so unfair," she said. "You look like *The Bourne Identity* and I look like *Big Trouble in Little China*."

I laughed. "What? I like the embroidered dragon on the back. It's cute. Now put this scarf over your head."

She jerked the red and purple crochet scarf from my hand. "Right, because I wasn't standing out enough already."

I took a few steps toward the end of the alley to scope out a car while she tied her scarf. When I turned back, another laugh escaped.

She crossed her arms, but the movement only made the material of her jacket puff up more. "It's not my fault," she said. "Tying scarfs was not covered in my mother's curriculum."

"It's fine," I said, reining in the laugher. "Let me." I unknotted the ball she'd formed beneath her chin and draped it over her head to wrap around and cross over the lower portion of her face.

When I finished, she was staring up at me. "Did you find us a new car?"

I gave her a questioning look.

"Because I was thinking, a truck might be better. Or a tank."

I shook my head. "That's not what we're using it for this time." I held the cell phone up. "I've got to make a call. When I'm done, keep up."

I couldn't help but smile at her baffled expression. I dialed Brendan's personal cell, the only one I was certain wouldn't be tracked.

He answered, "Go ahead."

"It's me," I said. I could almost hear the relief in his silence. "I need to bring something in."

"I've heard. Is she hurt?"

"No, but not for lack of trying."

"Should we pick you up?"

I glanced at Emily. "No. We'll make it to the drop point late tomorrow. Just get us from there."

"Got it. And Aern?"

I waited.

"Keep her safe."

The call disconnected and I read the screen. One full second ahead of a possible trace time. I didn't risk it.

I grabbed Emily's hand and headed for the car that was double-parked on the busy street, pushing her around the rear quarter as I dropped the cell into a crack in the open window. I crossed the street quickly and she followed as instructed, keeping tucked just behind me with her head down. I shoved my hands in my pockets and raised my shoulders as if I were chilled by the wind, then picked up my pace.

Several blocks later, I turned into the lobby of a busy hotel. I could see Emily follow in the reflection of the glass front windows.

"Look at the brochures," I said quietly. "I'll get us a room."

She stood in the foyer while I crossed the lobby to the elevators. I pressed the button twice and glanced up at the numbers above the door as any guest would. The first time it opened, a family of four went in.

I waved them on. "I'll grab the next one."

The little boy took the opportunity to slide his hand over the entire bottom half of the floor buttons. His mother smacked his fingers away and groaned.

A graying businessman sidled up beside me, chuckling at the scene. "Excuse me," I said, touching his forearm where it rested on the handle of his rolling suitcase.

Minutes later, I leaned around the corner and waved Emily over.

She glanced at the agitated businessman as she passed him on his way to the doors. "What's wrong with him?" she whispered.

"Bed bugs." I shrugged. "Said he was going to stay at the Marriott on Ninth."

Her face twisted.

"Don't worry," I told her. "The receptionist assured me it wasn't true."

She didn't look convinced, but before she could examine the distance between us and the reception desk, the elevator doors dinged open and I urged her in.

8

MR. SMITH

The keycard I'd swiped was to an executive queen on the fourth floor. Basically, this meant the room consisted of a lone bed, a dresser holding a small television, and a desk and chair with access to the internet. After where we'd been sleeping, it seemed like the Ritz. I didn't even bother checking the windows. At this level, and in this part of town, they'd be sealed. If anything were to happen here, we'd have to fight our way out.

I tugged off the jacket and tossed it on the bed, and then scratched my hair after taking the ball cap off. Emily was leaning over near the end of the bed, lifting the corner of a blue patterned comforter.

"What are you doing?"

She straightened, her face red and hair askew from being upside down. "Bed bugs."

I bit my cheek. "Why don't you go ahead and clean up. I'll check the bed."

She nodded, but then turned back on her way to the bathroom. "Is it safe?"

"Absolutely."

She narrowed her gaze on me for a moment, but the temptation of clean water won out.

I picked up the phone and pressed the room service key, trying to mimic the gruff voice of the man whose credit card was on file. I ordered a salad, a fruit plate, and then decided Emily was a cheeseburger girl. "Extra fries," I said. "And the cherry cheesecake."

As I returned the receiver to its cradle, I heard the water shut off in the shower. The bathroom door cracked open and in the reflection of the mirrored closet doors across the narrow entry hall, I could see Emily peek out through the opening.

"No one here but me," I said. "Still safe."

She didn't say anything, but the door clicked closed for another few minutes. When she emerged again, it was in bare feet. Her wet hair hung in dark waves over her dirty gray tee shirt, and her jeans were rolled up at the hems. She held the damp towel in her hands.

"Are you going to shower?"

"Nah." I smiled. "I've got a few more days."

She made a face as she pressed the towel to the ends of her damp hair. She absently glanced around the room, dark carpet, beige walls, generic still life painting over the bed, and then her eyes fell on me.

"Your arm," she said, suddenly recalling the injury.

I glanced down. "It's fine."

She crossed to me. "It's not fine." She leaned closer, examining the wound. Her eyes came up to mine.

"It's fine," I said again.

She took a corner of the damp towel and brushed a section of dried blood away. She swallowed, not able to look at me.

I took the towel from her hand. "I'll clean it up."

I stood to go rinse it in the sink and Emily backed up to sit numbly on the bed.

I left the door open as I washed the blood away. Nothing remained but a thin pink line. I wadded the towel and tossed it to the floor.

When I returned, Emily was still sitting motionless on the side of the bed near the nightstand. I would have to wait, I thought, tell her in the morning.

I sat beside her, but on the far end, and that was how we stayed, unspeaking, for the next twenty minutes. It was so still and quiet, I could actually hear her stop breathing when the impatient knocking echoed loudly through the room.

"It's okay," I said, reaching out to touch her forearm as I spoke. "Room service. I'm sorry, I should have told you."

She swallowed, and began breathing again. The bellman's knuckles rapped the door three more times.

I glanced through the peephole, but he was staring, annoyed, at the tray of food and not the door or the hall. I heard the bed creak behind me as I slid the chain, switched the lock, and opened the door. She was watching again.

"Good evening, Mister"—the bellman glanced at the tray—"Smith."

I winced.

"May I come in?"

"Please," I answered, moving out of his way only long enough to let him pass before securing the door once more.

He crossed to the desk and slid an extension out from the bottom. "Lovely weather this evening."

"Yes," I said. I grabbed the ticket from the tray as he removed the dish covers to display our dinner. I tipped him well, but not enough that he would mention it to anyone.

"Thank you, sir," he said, only nodding to Emily before heading for the door. "Have a wonderful stay."

I touched his shoulder as he passed. "Here," I said, brushing away his memories of the couple in 402. "Let me get the door for you."

He walked, slightly dazed, from the room, and then seemed to remember himself halfway down the hall.

"What?" Emily said from behind me.

I'd jumped. Again. "Nothing," I said. "Let's eat."

She peered out beside me in time to see the bellman enter

the service elevator. I pressed her back into the room and latched the door.

Emily stood staring at the plates of food, so I unrolled the napkin and handed her a fork. I kept the knife, and began cutting the sandwich in half, and she followed my example by dumping the condiment bowl and portioning out salad. There was only the one chair at the desk, so she moved the plates to the center of the bed, and climbed in to sit cross-legged by the headboard. I sat on the opposite side near the end, and picked up half a cheeseburger from our shared platter.

I was on my last bite when she said, "So... Mister Smith?"

Unprepared, I almost choked.

She smirked, quite nearly a smile, and bit into a French fry. "Where did you learn all of this?" she asked. "This cloak-and-dagger stuff?"

I laughed. "Cloak-and-dagger?"

She shrugged.

"I didn't," I said honestly. I picked up a grape and rolled it between thumb and forefinger. "This... this wasn't supposed to happen."

Emily leaned forward, and I regretted giving her any clue to the unreliability of the prophecy.

I dropped the grape. "I was never supposed to be on the run. Before all this, it never crossed my mind I'd be doing surveillance, or misleading Council, let alone protecting someone. It wasn't part of the plan."

"The plan?" she asked.

"They had it all figured out," I explained. "Taught us everything we'd need to know." I met Emily's eyes. "They trained us all right, just not for this."

"Us?"

"Morgan," I said. "Morgan and I were educated in the ways of the blood, learned in the ideals of Council."

"Morgan," she said, "he's the one I saw at the warehouse? He's your brother?"

I nodded. "My older brother. The first born."

"The chosen one," Emily whispered. She'd lost her appetite as well, dropping her last fry back to the plate.

"He came into this world knowing he would rule," I said, thinking of the devastation he would cause, of the thousands he would kill, of the rest he would send to war. Of the end of our lines. All for power. I let go of the thought, finding Emily once more. "When I came along a few years later, he decided I was to be his underling, that I should serve and bow to him." I wiped my hands on a napkin and tossed it onto the tray. "He feels he's owed this by Council, by all of us. Nothing in this life will ever convince him any differently. The idea of the prophecy has warped his sense of being, his principles."

Emily pulled her knees up tight, tucking her hands over her bare feet. "And so he's been waiting? All this time, searching for Brianna?"

A harsh laugh escaped. "He's not exactly been sitting idle,

no. Morgan has had an abundance of unpleasant pursuits in the years before we found her."

Emily sat up, suddenly rigid. "We?"

"Council," I said. "We of the blood." I stood to collect the tray. "But it was one of his minions who finally tracked her down."

"How did they know?" she asked. "How did they know, after all this time, to look for her?"

"It wasn't her at all," I said. "It was us. It was that a son was finally born to our line."

Emily paled, and I knew she was remembering the words of the prophecy. The prophecy that, not so long ago, had only been a fiction in her mind, the ramblings of an eccentric parent.

I gave her a moment to gather her thoughts as I slid the tray into the hall. When I returned, she was already recovered and waiting for me to continue.

I sat on the bed opposite her. "The prophecy says that 'a daughter of great power, born of the serpent with eyes of the sea, will bring absolute conflict'. That's not much to go on, really. So Council has been watching for the other clues. Namely, 'the heir to the dragon's name will rule with their union.' It doesn't seem like much, until you count the fact that the dragon hasn't had an heir in a few hundred years."

"I'm sorry," Emily said, "but my mother... Well, maybe she did explain it, but I guess I didn't really listen to everything she said. I just thought it didn't matter, that it was a story."

"Where did I lose you?"

"The dragon?" she asked.

"I don't suppose you could know that," I said. "A lot of the words in the prophecy actually mean something else. They were written in the old language, and even we don't reference things the same way now. The dragon points to my family's bloodline, one of the Seven. Those who had ruled in the past. And an 'heir to the name' is an unusual one, since names weren't even passed as such when the prophecy was written, but it says that the chosen one must be male."

"And there weren't any before?"

I shook my head. "Not for a very long time. The blood was passed mother to daughter until Morgan was born."

"How do you know?" she whispered. "I mean, how can you be sure?"

I shrugged. "Council has been studying the prophecy since before any of us were even born. I suppose we just trust them to understand the clues and hidden meanings."

"Have you seen it?" she asked.

I smiled. "Yes. Only me—they didn't trust Morgan with it."

She leaned closer. "Was it... Did you *know*?"

I leaned forward as well. "I did."

A sad smile crossed her lips as she leaned back against the headboard. "I wish I had seen it. I wish, so much, that something could have convinced me. That I could have believed her."

"You did," I said. "When it counted."

We sat silent for a moment, and I could see exhaustion take over Emily's features. I glanced at the brown plaid chair in the corner, and then brushed my hands over my jeans before standing to go to it.

Emily grabbed my arm. "Aern?"

I turned back to her.

"Tell me Brianna is safe."

"She is," I promised. "She will always be safe."

She drew me toward her, gaze dropping as she pressed me back on the pillows to curl against my chest. The motion was tentative, but she had done it nonetheless.

I wrapped my arm around her shoulder. "You will both be safe, Emily. I swear by it."

9

THE DIVISION

I stared at the toes of my boots until morning. I didn't look at the girl in my arms, at her honeyed locks that had dried, uncombed, into loose ribbons. I didn't watch the skin of her bare arm, draped easily across my cotton-covered abdomen, or the way her lips occasionally twitched while she slept, tucked neatly into the crook of my arm.

And I certainly didn't think about the way her cheek felt, pressed to my chest. At least, not until she began to wake.

A quiet rumble came from deep in her throat and she burrowed deeper into my shirt before the arm wrapped across my middle drew in and then unbent over me in a stretch. The rest of her body followed, both legs straightened out, her bare feet pointed to the black television screen across the room.

And then her eyes shot open.

I smiled at her stunned face as she stared up at me, only inches away.

She kept her gaze on me, but pulled her arm back, hand half open as she decided whether to press my chest in order to raise off me. I made no move to ease her escape. This close, I could see each of her dark lashes, the faintest of freckles on her cheekbones, the curve of her lip...

She swallowed hard, and then abruptly remembered herself and rolled back and onto her knees. "Aern." It came out breathier than she intended and she quickly cleared her throat.

"Sleep well?" I asked, leaning forward to move my feet to the floor.

She seemed unsure for a moment and then relaxed, stretched again, and decided, "Yes."

When it appeared she was going to ask me the same, I said, "How do you like your eggs?"

This threw her again, but she finally answered, "Scrambled." And then, "Thanks."

I walked around the bed to call in our breakfast order, and Emily made her way to the bathroom. As I raised the handset to my ear, I found the closet mirror opposite her and was distracted from my task.

She paused in front of the sink, looking incredulously at her reflection. Her lips formed some silent words that I couldn't make out, though I tried, and then they stilled, pursed, then relaxed. She sighed deep, rubbed a hand numbly over her cheek, and turned to reach for the door. Our eyes met, and for one brief moment, she watched me watch her.

And then she closed the door.

I ended my call to the sound of her fumbling with the coffee maker. I crossed to the window and drew the curtains and shades fully open to stare out into the city. It was early, and the sun cast a rich amber glow against the haze. The light threw shadows behind the tallest buildings, banks and corporate offices, completely unaware of the looming apocalypse. So many of them. Oblivious to the prophecy, to the war we were fighting to save us all. They didn't keep their history, didn't know of Council's wish to return to the way things were. When our kind held dominion over all. They didn't even know we existed. If Morgan succeeded, they would think him merely another human.

Until the killing began.

"Coffee?" Emily offered from beside me.

I took the cup, and then struck by the sight of her in the early morning sun, forgot myself.

She pretended not to notice as she turned to face the window. Her hair was tucked behind her ear and she wore three-day-old clothes, but she'd straightened them both, and her cheeks wore a thin layer of softly scented lotion.

"Thank you," I said. She looked at me as if she wasn't sure

why I was thanking her, and I raised the coffee. She nodded absently. "Not a morning person?" I asked.

An undecipherable huff escaped her. "I guess not." She shook her head, thoughts elsewhere. And then, "So, about that phone call yesterday." She glanced down at her cup; her thumb flicked anxiously at the mug's grip. "You're going to drop me off at a safe house?"

"We'll talk about that," I said. "But after breakfast."

A knock sounded at the door and Emily's head quirked to the side, birdlike, as she speculated how I'd predicted it. I sat my cup on the desk as if it wasn't out of the ordinary at all, and retrieved the tray from the bellman without letting him in.

We ate in silence and Emily finished before I'd made it halfway through my food. She sat in the plaid corner chair, napkin covering her empty plate, and hands crossed over one another in her lap. I sat in the desk chair, trying to ignore her impatient stare while I buttered my second slice of toast.

As I took the last bite and wiped my hands on a napkin, she straightened, rigid with attentiveness. I stood to move her plate and my own back to the tray before turning to her.

"I'm not taking you to the safe house," I said. "I'm taking you to your sister."

The force with which she leapt from the chair and launched herself at me was incredible, and I nearly staggered back into the desk, dishes and all. Instead, I stood in shock, her arms wrapped tightly around me in a hug so fierce it was disarming.

She was gasping, and I gripped her shoulders to push her away, just enough to see her face. "Emily, there's something you need to know…"

But she was crying.

Her wide, green eyes glistened with moisture as she looked up at me with unfathomable hope and relief washing her features. "Emily," I repeated, and one tear escaped the outside corner of her eye, tracing slowly down her cheek. I brushed it away with a thumb and my chest tightened. What was I doing?

"Emily," I said firmly.

She nodded dazedly and made an effort to pull herself together. She shook herself, and suddenly her eyes were dry, clear when they met mine again. "Something I need to know?"

She said the words, but I didn't think they'd fully registered. "About where I'm taking you," I explained. "About… the Division."

As quickly as her embrace had sprung upon me, it was gone. I felt suddenly bereft, and it was dizzying, alien. She had moved back, never taking her eyes off me, face blank with shock that was swiftly turning to horror.

"The Division?" she whispered, and it was unclear if the words were meant to question me or convince herself of what she'd heard. Either way, she didn't believe it. Didn't *want* to believe it.

"She's safe, Emily. They won't hurt her. It was the only way—"

"You took my sister to the Division?" she hissed.

"I had no other choice. They are the only ones I could trust with her."

She looked sick. And afraid. Her gaze flicked to the door and I stepped sideways toward the bed, hands up in the palms-out gesture reserved for wild animals, in my attempt to block her long enough to explain. I threw everything in my sway toward her, pleading for calm, and for a moment, I thought it worked. Until she had a knife point aimed at my chest.

"Don't," I said tightly, battling with anger that I'd left a weapon within her reach and alarm at the speed at which she'd retrieved it.

She didn't speak, but I could see she was measuring her options. Suddenly her questions the previous night took on new meaning and I couldn't help but wonder about her own "education."

My stance adjusted to more of a ready crouch. It was only a serrated stainless blade, but I was quickly becoming aware of her capabilities. She had eluded Morgan's men. Certainly they wouldn't have considered her a threat, merely another human, easily swayed. But she had still managed to find us, walk herself into that warehouse. His warehouse.

The lingering pain in my shoulder became a niggling distraction.

"Let me past," she said in an unsteady voice.

"You can't, Emily. Let me explain—"

"Let me past," she repeated, though this time it was saturated with hatred and despair.

"You'll never find them," I said. "Not without me."

She considered that for less than a second before tightening her grip on the knife. "There is no *with you*."

I hadn't expected her to know the Division. But the revulsion in her words made me wonder if she knew more than I. "I have to keep Brianna safe," I said. "I will do whatever that requires."

She narrowed her gaze on me.

"You can't do this."

"Stop me," she said, and I could see her decide to make a move.

"I won't let you," I warned. "I can't—"

Emily rushed me. Her moves were swift and sure, and left no doubt she'd been training for most of her life. She might not have believed her mother, but she had certainly paid attention in class.

Her knife bit at me with quick, short dives between practiced leg sweeps and palm thrusts. She kept herself low, as small a target as possible, and free from my grasp. She knew I wouldn't hurt her, or didn't care, and worked to use my size against me. All I could do without injuring one of us was avoid her strikes.

She feigned left, and then darted right, but instead of stabbing at me flipped the tray, dishes and all, at my upper body. It should have given her the opportunity to slip by, but I was no back-alley mugger. I got a secure grip on her arm and swung her around, her back toward me, to grab the other.

I had her trapped by a firm hold on each arm, just above the elbow where I had the best leverage, and the knife fell to the floor. For half a second, I thought that meant she'd given up, but she drew her bare feet together over it and thrust toward my thigh without pause. I dodged the blow, but she'd lost her footing so my movement dropped her to kneeling. She tried to roll forward and catch me off balance and it nearly worked, but I was not physically unsteady, merely thrown by her maneuvers. By the idea that she—Emily—could fight this well.

I pulled her from the floor and she drew her legs up fluidly before kicking out to shove off the dresser and propel herself into me. I struggled to hold her. It was not unlike holding a cat. Some wild, ninja, cat.

I braced myself, legs wide, and drew her against me to twist her arms securely within mine. I pressed a hand to her neck to prevent her from smashing my face with the back of her skull and said evenly, "Emily, I don't want to hurt you."

It was probably mostly true.

She didn't speak, simply raised her legs from the floor, forcing me to hold all of her weight. I sighed.

"Give," I said. "Give and have a conversation with me or so help me—"

My threat was cut short as her bare right foot shot out to connect with the corner of the flatscreen television. I caught the move just in time to save her from flipping it toward us and spun around to throw her onto the bed. She'd no more than had a chance to roll over before I was on her, pinning her down on all points beneath me. She jerked, but it was too late, I had her. I sat atop her hips, my knees pinning her forearms while my legs, bent behind me, trapped her just above the knees.

Were she able to move, my free hands could discourage the notion, but she wasn't, so I simply sat there, staring down at her, reminding her that she never had a chance.

She was furious. I wasn't sure exactly when she'd lost her cool, but her cheeks were flushed and her jaw tight. Her hair had gone wild, splayed over the mussed blue comforter behind her. Her chest heaved, both her and the bed covered in bits of scrambled egg. Spots of something dark had splattered her shirt. I felt a tug at the corner of my mouth, but the look in her eye told me I was about to get an earful of something.

I'd never know exactly what though, because, suddenly, three loud knocks rang through the room and the atmosphere transformed entirely.

10

EGGS AND BLOOD

Emily abandoned all signs of struggle. She steadied her breathing, face nothing but alert, when a woman on the other side of the door said, "Housekeeping."

There was no way to know whether we were in danger, or I might have left it be. But this woman might have heard the struggle, the crashing dishes, might have been listening from the hall for some time.

I leaned forward, questioning Emily's compliance with my eyebrows, but she didn't move.

I slid from the bed, but hesitated as my shoes touched carpet. I didn't quite trust her.

"Stay," I said levelly, walking backward to the entry. She

simply stared at me, looking past the finger pointing her down, and breathed.

The maid waited impatiently on the other side of the door. Mr. Smith's room had been marked for early checkout, she explained. I told her there'd been a slight change of plans, but gave her my assurance she'd have the room within an hour or so. By the time the maid had moved on to clean a room down the hall, Emily had composed herself and sat on the edge of the bed, picking egg from her shirt and hair.

I leaned against the dresser across from her, and then folded my arms over my chest when I realized the dark splatters covering her were blood, where she'd nicked my forearms. The wounds had already begun to close, and I didn't need to add that particular detail to our discourse. I gritted my teeth. Who sent a steak knife for scrambled eggs, anyway?

Emily looked up at me.

"I know you're upset," I said. "But there is more to all of this than your sister." I didn't know if she understood that, if her mother had explained the full extent of the prophecy, that the union would decide who ruled, whether or not the game-ending war would play through, but she didn't react at all to my words. "I had no choice but to take her there. I'll try to explain it to you, as much as I can, but I can't let you go, not now."

She didn't argue, but I recognized a "why" in her expression.

"They are searching for you now, Emily. Morgan's men will find you, they will do anything to get to you."

The idea distracted me, and my hands fell to the dresser to curl over the edge I leaned against. Emily noticed the short stripes of dry blood and looked a little sick.

"I'm sorry," I said automatically, and then realized how ridiculous it was. I rubbed a palm surreptitiously over the worst patch to brush it loose and changed my apology into what it should have been for. "You should have never been involved. If Morgan were to find you, he could pull anything you've learned from your mind." Her eyes came back to mine. "And I've already let you know more than is safe."

"Morgan," she asked, "he's different... from the others?"

I nodded. "He's stronger. There's never been a commonblood immune to his gift."

She swallowed. "And Brianna, she's not immune?"

"We don't know," I said truthfully. "He's not had the chance to try."

Emily chewed her lip, contemplating this for a very long time before she finally spoke again. "I'll go with you. I'll go to save Brianna."

She moved to stand, but I stopped her. "Not yet."

"We have to go now," she insisted.

"There are a few things I need to explain first."

Her lips were moving in that measured, silent way again, the way they had as the policemen searched for us outside the warehouse. The way they had as she climbed the hotel. I knelt before her, finally able, to some degree, to read her lips and gather a few words. *A prophecy.*

I was suddenly standing again. She was reciting words in the ancient language, re-memorizing a prophecy. Not our prophecy, but her own. My heart sank in a *why me* kind of hopelessness as Emily realized my discovery. She looked at once guilty and defiant.

"Tell me," I said flatly.

Her fingers curled into her palms. "I don't know," she stammered. "I can't remember. There were so many." She glanced up at me again, stricken. "And I didn't pay attention. I didn't believe her, Aern."

"Your mother?"

She nodded.

"Your mother was a prophet," I repeated, to no one in particular.

"I didn't know," she said.

They were wrong about the prophecy. All this time, it wasn't a daughter of great power, but the daughter of *a* great power. Did that mean Brianna truly wasn't hiding a talent as the Division had suspected? Did it mean they were wrong about her protector as well?

"What did she say, Emily?"

Emily shook her head. "Something about the Division. The Taken will die at the hands of the Division." She pressed her fingers to her temples, desperately seeking the words. "I can't remember it all. But the Division is bad, Aern. She drilled that into my head over and over and over. We've got to get her out of there."

"They won't kill her," I promised. "They have to keep her alive. They have to keep her from the Council."

"But—"

"That's why she's there," I said. "They need her."

"No," she said. "No, that's not right. Why would they need Brianna?"

My jaw flexed involuntarily. "To get me."

Emily's mouth went slack with confusion and I sat heavily beside her. "That's what I wanted to tell you about," I said. "Why the Division is after me."

11

MORALS

Emily sat silent while I attempted to explain my relationship with the Division, how I'd handed her sister over to the one group her prophecy said would kill her. I told her how Morgan had turned on us. How he'd removed all those of Council who didn't cower to him. I explained our fear, that those who stayed seemed to submit to his every whim, as if they'd lost their own power of will. I told her he was treacherous, barbaric, but I didn't tell her the extent of his cruelty. I didn't tell her of the human girls we'd found, their bodies barely recognizable, as he passed the time until he came into his prophesied power. I couldn't tell her that. Not when he was after her, and not when he was after Brianna.

"Brendan convinced the others to leave Council, and he's been gathering new followers every day." Every time Morgan committed a new offense. "The split is quickly becoming a war. I'd never officially left Council, I stayed to try and right things, and I stayed because it was my place. When it went beyond fixing, I simply stepped away from everyone. The Division has been wooing me for a long time," I said. "But I've never had to take sides."

"Until Brianna," she said weakly.

"It was all I could do. The best place for her. No one there will want any harm to come to her. Their entire goal revolves around her."

"And then why," she asked, "if they want you so bad, if Morgan is so terrible, why don't you join them?"

"I don't trust them."

"You don't trust them?"

"I won't tell you why. I can't tell you, because there's still a chance——" I couldn't finish. I couldn't tell her how close we were to harm, how there was no guarantee of keeping either of us out of Morgan's hands completely. I couldn't tell her about the Division's interpretation of the prophecy, that they wanted me because they planned to use the second heir to the name for the foretold union. I said, "They don't want me for the right reasons, Emily. And I don't want you to trust them either."

She'd lost her determination again, her hands fisted to stop the trembling.

"They will protect her. It's the safest place in the world for her right now. And by this afternoon, we'll be with her." She nodded and I turned her to look directly into her eyes. "Don't trust them, Emily. Stay with Brianna."

She agreed to do as I asked, but I couldn't help reminding her again as she laced her shoes and found her jacket. I didn't tell her why, that if Brendan or any of the others were somehow able to penetrate her mind in a way I couldn't seem to do, Brianna would know. Brianna could stop them. But as I glanced around the room, I thought maybe I'd wasted my breath, because Emily didn't trust them at all. She'd been told her whole life they would kill her sister. And now I was forcing her to ally with them, to stay under their protection. I shook my head.

Emily stepped beside me and stared at the shattered dishes strewn across the room, assuming I was shaking my head at the mess she'd made. She glanced at me, silently questioning whether she needed to pick it up, and broke my contemplation. I found the receipt among the chaos and signed for the charge. She'd just cost Mr. Smith a pretty big tip.

We left the hotel to much warmer weather. Emily squinted against the sunlight, and her hand slipped beneath my arm to wrap loosely over my wrist as we navigated the crowd outside the valet stand. Several taxis waited for guests checking out, but we walked past them, opting instead for a random cab passing by several blocks from the hotel.

"Where to?" the driver asked, barely glancing at us as Emily slid into the back seat.

"Harper's Park, please."

His eyes met mine in the rear view mirror and I could see the corners wrinkle up with a knowing smile. Harper's had a reputation, it was a famed makeout spot for the city kids with no place to meet up. I wagged my eyebrows at him and draped an arm over the seat behind Emily.

It was only then that I noticed her staring incredulously at the exchange. I grinned and shrugged my free shoulder as if to say, *Cloak-and-dagger, baby*. She rolled her eyes.

We drove through the city in silence, Emily studying every car at every street, tensing each time we were passed. I couldn't tell if she was anxious to finally be this close to Brianna, or if it was the Division.

I touched the gold satin of her jacket to get her attention. "Will it help if I tell you she's fine?"

"No," she said. "I just have to see for myself."

"A few hours," I promised, and she took a deep breath.

When the cab pulled up to the curb at Harper's, I drew Emily out behind me and slid my hand through the side window as if I were passing a folded bill to the driver. "Keep the change," I said offhandedly, using my sway to convince him the bill was actually there.

Emily was inspecting the park during the exchange, and when I straightened to let the cab pull away, I slipped a hand on her lower back and ushered her through one of the gates.

It was far from a casual stroll, but we kept pace with the other park inhabitants so as not draw any undue attention. Birds chirped, picnickers lounged, and a few cyclists spun past as we silently made our way across the park. Sunlight dappled the walkway, broken only by the shadow of cottonwood leaves. The path turned over a low bridge and two geese drifted slowly beneath us. It was all wrong.

Emily walked beside me, hands shoved in her jacket pockets, eyes pinched at the corners. Clearly, she wasn't feeling the peaceful atmosphere, either.

We came out of the park on the south side of Grant Street. The sidewalk was lined with vendors setting up for the afternoon rush. It was here that I rented the scooter.

"No," Emily said as I passed her the half helmet and goggles.

"They'll help disguise you."

"Not that." She shoved the proffered helmet aside and pointed at the scooter. "That."

I shook my head and threw a leg over the tiny red machine. "Women."

"What—" she stammered. "Did you just—"

I smiled.

She narrowed her eyes and yanked the helmet out of my hands. I had to look away when she shoved it down over all that hair and her vicious glare disappeared behind dark goggles. She muttered something nasty when she wrapped her arms around my chest and realized I was laughing, but I couldn't hear it over the tinny rev of the engine as we sped away.

Normally, a moped was not an ideal getaway car. But as we slipped quickly between traffic and down alleys, I was sure even Emily had forgiven the unusual selection. There was a festival on Sixth and Market Street, and the area was crowded with pedestrians. I felt Emily's grip tighten on my chest, and took us two blocks south before heading back toward our destination. We walked the final three blocks to the Carlson hotel after leaving the scooter leaned against a café railing.

At the Carlson, we entered through the parking garage to walk out the front doors of the hotel as guests. We didn't look the part, but no one argued as we slid into one of the waiting town cars.

"Fordham Heights," I instructed the driver, not missing the sidelong glance Emily gave me. She must know the place, and there was no question she was surprised at the direction our journey was headed. I figured it best to get it all out of the way now.

"Aside from our discussion earlier," I asked, "what do you know of our friends?"

She stared at me blankly for a moment, and then swallowed. "Not much."

I nodded. "One more thing you should know, that you should expect, is that they've been very successful."

"You mean…"

"Their special insight into the business world, their relationship with powerful people, it has allowed them to garner ample property, funds, and the like."

She quirked one brow at my talking in code, but it fell when she realized what I was telling her. The Division used their sway to cheat and steal their way to riches. And then she glanced at my days-old shirt, still no worse for wear, the cut of my jeans.

"It's another value we don't share," I said. "I earn what I have." Aside from the last few days, I thought. But Morgan hadn't given me much choice.

"I didn't…"

I waved a hand. "Don't worry about it. I just want you to understand. To know what to expect. The rest of us don't use our advantage for arrangements, we're honest businessmen."

"All of you?" Emily whispered.

I sighed. "We were. It seems both sides are now led by the selfish, their greed and want for power." I spun the ring on my middle finger. "Morals are not a tool for war."

Emily smiled. It was just the tiniest rise of her lips and it was gone as quickly as it had appeared, but it was a smile. "You sound like my sensei," she said.

The driver dropped us at Fordham Heights and we walked toward the train station. Emily questioned my methods, but realized quickly that any pursuers would be easier to spot if they'd managed to follow us through so many different routes.

"Council trained us how to respond," I said. "All of us. And so we can't use those techniques. We have to decide on the spur of the moment, be as unpredictable as possible."

"Sorry," she said. "I'm just anxious to see Brianna." She glanced down the stairwell. "And I hate trains."

I smiled. "Me too, but that's not where we're headed."

There wasn't much else around Fordham, no taxis, no bike rentals. She looked up at me, brows raised. "It's not?"

I spun her toward the street, where a black limousine waited curbside. "Nope." And then I leaned in to whisper in her ear, "And it's bulletproof. Like a tank."

She smiled, and this time it was for real.

12

Reunions

The ride to the estate was brief, and Emily sat eagerly beside me peering out the tinted glass. When the driver slowed to turn into a security gate, she squeezed the crook of my arm. It wasn't until we'd passed through and began to spot the gardens and outbuildings that I realized she wasn't letting go.

It was hard not to be impressed by the white, marble-columned mansion, somehow both stately and modern at once. The design was timeless, materials priceless, and Emily barely seemed to notice. A security guard opened the door as we came to a stop, and Emily climbed over me to push by him.

As soon as her feet hit the pavement, she was running for the house. She didn't even notice the red Ferrari on her way past, or the four guards in Armani suits placed outside the main door. But it didn't matter, because as soon as she'd reached the top step, Brianna came running toward her.

They hit with a practiced familiarity, and held each other for several long breaths before Emily's hands moved to grab Brianna's shoulders and push her back, just far enough to glare at her. I'd made it within earshot when Brianna whispered, "It was the only way."

I could see the tension slowly leave Emily's shoulders. And then Brianna reached a hand up to cup her sister's cheek. "Em, you slept." Emily eased out of the embrace a little more and Brianna laughed. "And what are you wearing?"

Emily glared at her. "I didn't have a lot of time to prepare."

Brianna smiled sweetly. "You know I have some things for you."

"You always do," Emily said, sliding free of the hug to finally take in her surroundings.

From the open door, Brendan smiled past the reunion to me. "Good to have you back, brother. We weren't sure a time or two." Emily stiffened at the remark, but it was only a meaningless word, meant to secure our bond, and no doubt a surreptitious jab at Morgan.

I nodded toward him in acknowledgement, but before I could respond, Brianna was rushing me.

"Aern," she gushed. "Thank you for keeping her safe." I smiled, but Brianna had gripped my arms while speaking, and she noticed the partially healed cuts marking them. She said, "Oh, Aern, you're hurt."

Emily had the decency to look chagrined, but when I smiled at her, she narrowed her eyes, daring me to tell.

"It's nothing," I told Brianna.

She ran her hands over my arms, and I wondered at how thin and pale she seemed. It might have just been that I'd gotten used to Emily, that her vitality had exaggerated the difference between the two, but I couldn't remember thinking Brianna had looked anything but slim before.

Brendan cleared his throat. "Maybe we should continue this reunion inside."

Brianna rolled her eyes and smiled at me before turning to face him. "They'll need some food and hot tea. I'll take Emily up for a bath, you should have hers served to my room. Something light, I'm sure they've had a rough morning."

Brendan's mouth tightened, but he bent his head in acquiescence.

As the girls walked through the door, his eyes narrowed at my silent laughter. I shook my head. "I take it she's figured out she's useful to you."

"No thanks to you, I'm sure," he muttered.

I scratched my stomach. "Fetch my tea, Brendan. I'll be in the bath." His elbow caught me in the ribcage as we crossed the threshold and I couldn't help but laugh.

Emily glanced over her shoulder at the noise, and our eyes stayed locked as she climbed the last few stairs on Brianna's arm. I sighed. It was probably the last time I'd see that gold silk jacket.

13

HEALING

The Division had set up a suite of rooms for me at three of their most frequented houses. This one however, was the smallest and safest, and as such not normally filled with eight of their top men. Brendan had offered me a better room, but I'd chosen an empty one close to Brianna and Emily.

Not that it was lacking. A king-size bed lay centered among a space twice the size of our last hotel room, all cream and black, clean and classic. The walls were bare aside from a small metal sculpture between the walk-in closet and the private bath. I kicked off my shoes at the end of the bed and walked over plush cream carpet to the bathroom, which could be called nothing but opulent. No doubt the stone was imported and hand-carved, glass surrounds custom and one of a kind. I shook my head and tossed my dirty shirt onto the counter.

As I reached for the faucet, I noticed the skin of my forearm appeared too smooth. It had, only a short time ago, still bore the raised pink lines of a jagged half-healed cut. But now, without sleep, the wound was all but gone. I squinted against the dim mood lighting in the shower room, and drew the arm closer. And then I winced, because my shoulder had apparently not had time to heal. I rubbed a hand over my face and turned the shower on full and hot before dropping both arms to tilt my head back and just stand there in the spray.

It must have been an hour later when I finally lay down. I had come out of the shower to find sandwiches and hot tea waiting on the bureau, as well as a clean set of clothes. I had pulled the jeans on while I ate, and then fell into bed, shirtless and sock-footed, to at last get the sleep I needed for my shoulder to heal.

So I was feeling better by the time movement in my room woke me. I didn't have to open my eyes to know it was Emily.

I lay on top of a satin duvet, not having bothered with removing the mass of pillows at the head of the bed, face down with one arm slung over the side. She leaned over, holding her breath as she scrutinized the results of her handiwork on my arm. But the wounds would be undetectable by now.

"You shouldn't sneak up on people while they're sleeping," I said, snatching her wrist as she gasped and tried to jerk back from me.

She froze, free hand pressed to her heaving chest, and stared at me, wide-eyed. I pulled her closer. "What are you doing, Emily?"

She swallowed. "I was just... Sorry, I'll go."

I dragged her arm with me as I rolled to my back, forcing her to either perch awkwardly on the edge of the bed, or climb over me and stay. She chose the latter, carefully stepping clear of me to sit cross-legged by my hip.

"Where's Brianna?" I asked.

"Asleep."

"And you weren't tired?"

Emily bit her lip. "I can't really sleep." She glanced down at my bare torso, then quickly away, scanning the room for anything else to look at.

I released her arm. And then, recalling what Brianna had said at their reunion, asked, "You don't sleep much?"

"Hardly ever," she said, eyes coming back to me as I lay so similarly to the way I had in the hotel when she'd settled into my chest and slept through the night. "I've never been able to, not for more than an hour or so at a time."

Surely that had nothing to do with her mother training her to keep watch over her sister, telling her someone was after her, that she had to keep her safe.

But it was true, wasn't it?

"How is she?" I asked.

The corner of her mouth raised in a half-smile. "Brianna's fine. She's always fine." Emily twisted her hands together. "I just feel better seeing her, knowing she's safe."

"Emily," I said, "will anyone be looking for you?"

"You mean like our foster parents? No, no, I don't think we'll be missed. He'll get pretty worked up about his car, but he won't risk calling the law or losing his credibility with the system." She rubbed a hand absently up her arm. "Besides, if he even reports it to the agency, we'll be eighteen next week. It's not like they can do anything about it then."

"Was it only him?"

"Yeah. His wife ran off a while back, but he never admitted it to anyone. Thought they'd take us, I guess. It was better that way anyhow. Brianna couldn't stand to watch him hurt her."

I bit down hard to keep from speaking. It was none of my business. None of my business.

Emily realized what she'd said. "He never touched us," she promised. "I wouldn't have let him. But he wasn't a good man." She pressed her lips together. "It was just that we couldn't risk leaving, being separated. Not again. He stayed clear of Brianna, and I endured his words. So we could be together." She shrugged. "It didn't seem like that long to suffer."

He was the least of her troubles now, and it was obvious she was done talking about it, so I moved on. "What about school?"

She huffed out a breath akin to a laugh. "No, we tested out of school a long time ago. It wasn't all nunchakus and divinations. I can give you the square root of pi." She watched me for a moment, expression still.

I gave her a small smile. "We concentrated mostly on physics. And proper use of a screwdriver."

Her lips split into a grin, and I thought it was the first genuine happiness I'd seen from her. The idea tightened my chest a bit and I found myself making a promise there was no guarantee I could keep. A promise I had no right to make. "We'll figure it out, Emily. We'll take care of Morgan and Brianna will be safe. Even if I have to do it myself, she will be protected."

She was silent for a moment, considering my words. And then she whispered, "Thank you. Thank you for caring what happens to her."

I knew what she meant. Protecting Brianna could cost my people more than anything we'd lost in the past. But neither of us mentioned the rest of the prophecy, the fact that the fate of the human world hung in peril, or that the remainder of my kind could disappear forever. I simply pulled her into my arms and pressed my lips gently to the top of her head where it rested over my chest.

Even if I had to do it myself. Brianna would be safe.

The idea seemed to cost me something now, with her sister asleep in my arms, but it was looking to be the only way to keep Brianna from both sides of a war.

14

LUCK

When a knock sounded at the door later, we were both asleep. Emily jolted, but I squeezed her against me. "Yes?"

"We'll be serving dinner in half an hour, Mr. Archer."

"Fine." His footsteps didn't recede. "Thank you, Wesley."

"Sir..." He hesitated. "The girl, Miss Drake." He stopped again, realizing there were two Drake girls now. "Emily, sir..."

Emily's back stopped rising and falling beneath my hand and I had to bite back a smile. "Yes?"

"She's not in her room, sir. Should I report it to Brendan?"

I could hear the dread in his voice. No one wanted to give

Brendan bad news. "No, Wesley, she's fine. I'll see that she makes it to dinner."

"Thank you, sir. Thank you."

Wesley was skinny, awkward, and terrified of displeasing anyone in the Division. He was also trustworthy, efficient, and talented, but he'd been only fourteen when Morgan had first "reprimanded" him for a few minor slipups while working for Council. It had stuck with him, even after Brendan had taken him in. But Morgan had that effect on people.

Emily started breathing again. She pushed herself to sitting and I resisted the urge to drag her back, close my eyes, and fall asleep once more. I was glad my eyes were open when I saw her mortified expression.

I rose to my elbows. "Do you want to skip dinner?"

That only made it worse. Her cheeks reddened.

"All right, then. Why don't you sneak off to your sister's room and I'll meet you down there. I'm sure she's just about got the run of the place by now."

She moved to climb over me and I sat the rest of the way up, grasping her arm to stop her. We were face to face, inches apart when I whispered my warning. "Remember what I said, Emily. Stay with Brianna. I don't want you alone with any of them."

Slightly short of breath, she asked, "Even Brendan?"

Especially Brendan, I thought, but merely nodded.

I released my grip and swung my legs to the floor, sitting on the edge of the bed to watch her go. When the door clicked quietly shut behind her, I finally stretched my shoulder, grateful it had fully healed. It was the most I'd slept since Council had located Brianna.

I probably would have relaxed a few more minutes, but dinner would be set shortly, and I had some catching up to do. I slipped on my shoes and the button-up shirt that had been left out for me, not at all surprised to find it tailored to fit, before heading down to find Brendan. He would have been expecting me hours ago.

When I made it to the end of the hall, I was intercepted by an attractive brunette in her early twenties. "Oh, Mr. Archer, Mr. Samuels will want to see you."

"That's where I was headed," I explained. "Is Brendan in his office?"

"Yes," she said, "Mr. Samuels is in the front office suite, I'll take you there."

I smiled at her curt reminder of propriety, but it was received by the back of her head as she'd promptly spun to deliver me to the Mr. Samuels in question. She was dressed in a fitted navy jacket that had to have been custom-made, matching skirt falling exactly one inch above the knee. Her heels must have been padded to not echo off the wood floor, and only the swish of fabric accompanied us on our way, because she obviously had nothing to say to the likes of me.

We crossed through two beige rooms, and one more like creamed coffee, before arriving at Brendan's office. It was all mahogany and glass.

"Aern," he said, ignoring the brunette as she soundlessly stepped aside and backed from the room. "What kept you?"

If he knew, his face didn't betray it. "Catching up on some rest," I said, stretching my shoulder again for emphasis.

He walked around the desk to stand close, unbuttoning and rolling the cuffs of his shirt as he did so. "And I'm glad you did. Walk with me, will you?"

As we entered the hall, I raised a brow at him.

He shrugged. "I'm sure it's secure. It's just that lately I've been having trouble keeping things from our Brianna."

I tilted my head forward, not liking where this was going.

"No, no, I'm certain it's nothing," he said after seeing my response. "Maybe she isn't even aware of what's happening. It just seems like she's familiar with far too much." He rubbed a hand absently over his chest as we rounded the corner. "Things have been excitable around here to say the least. Probably one of the younger ones, they are so worked up about the actual prophecy girl being here. Likely one of them mentioned something they'd overheard from a private meeting."

I glanced over at him. "Prophecy girl?"

He smirked. "Yeah, that's what they're calling her. She's like a pop star around here."

"I've noticed I'm not getting the same reception," I said.

Brendan didn't meet my gaze. "They feel betrayed. Now that she's here, it's different. It's like you're refusing her, like you're refusing the prophecy."

"It isn't my prophecy."

"And so you'll leave her to Morgan?"

His words were ice and I stopped to stare at him. "Then you've turned on me as well."

"No," he said, letting out a deep breath. "No, Aern. It's... it's only that things have changed now. This is building to something we can't control. If we don't strike now—"

I cut him off, throwing his own words back at him. "I know the stakes, brother."

He held up a hand in forfeit. "You're right. We've had this argument enough. Come; let's update you on what you've missed."

I followed Brendan to a balcony overlooking several manicured acres that fell into dense woods. It was still cool, but he left the double doors open behind us, and if I hadn't known better, I'd have said we were alone. But there would be armed guards throughout the house, and though I couldn't spot them from this vantage point, I was certain the trees were crowded with even heavier security.

When Brendan leaned against the thick wood rail, I asked, "What have they learned?"

"They made the connection right away, traced the car back to their foster parents. The woman, she's safe as of this evening. As luck would have it, she'd changed her name, cut all ties to her previous life. They may track her down one day, but we'll keep an eye on things. The foster father, however, was not so fortunate. Morgan's men took him in the same day. Word is they botched their chance to get information from him, roughed him up a bit more than they should have."

I winced. When Morgan was angry, he tended to overdo the sway, let a little too much of his rage through.

Brendan nodded. "We had a team extract him, but it doesn't look good."

"Where is he?"

"Logan dropped him at County General, convinced him he'd been cleaning gutters when he'd fallen from the second-story roof and tumbled through the balcony railing before landing face first on the concrete drive. That should just about cover his injuries with the doctors, excepting the screw holes through his wrists."

I loosened my grip on the railing and turned to lean against it, watching the cream-colored curtains swim on the breeze.

"The house was clean," Brendan continued. "It had to have been dumb luck that they found you again."

"You're giving luck a lot of credit, Brendan."

He stared out over the lawn. "Maybe not luck so much. Maybe it's that the bastard turned a hundred men to find you."

Just then, one of the sheer curtains flipped in the wind and I caught sight of Emily across the expanse that was the dining hall. She held my eyes for one brief moment before a ribbon of beige fell between us.

Brendan looked over his shoulder, and I wondered if I'd given some clue to their arrival.

A trim blonde appeared a moment later, announcing his guests. "Thank you, Ellin," he said, distractedly scratching his jaw.

We pushed off the railing at the same time, walking in as Ellin discreetly closed the balcony doors behind us, and found Brianna and Emily standing beside a table set for fifteen. Brianna's eyes were trained on Brendan.

"You're not making a show of her," she said, somewhere between a demand and a question. It was clear the idea had her horrified.

"They're here for Aern, Brianna, not Emily." His gazed moved to Emily as he spoke. "And you do look lovely this evening, Miss Drake."

I had the distinct feeling it was meant as a spur for Brianna, but Emily ran a tense hand over the fabric of her blouse. I couldn't tell if she was uncomfortable with Brendan's attention, or having been outfitted in clothes that probably cost more than the last car she'd stolen.

Several key members of the Division came through the west door then, and the over-large room suddenly felt too full. Brendan took a moment to quickly present each of them to Emily, making a point not to allow them enough time in between introductions for more than a brief greeting.

The rest of the party filtered in and were fleetingly acknowledged before Brendan said, "Shall we?" and the group dispersed to find their seats. The head of the long table was left open for Brendan, who pulled out the chair to his left for Brianna. Emily watched the gesture with unveiled disapproval, and then ignored the chair that one of the staffers drew out for her to sit on Brianna's other side.

I was distracted from the scene by a light touch on my forearm, Ellin indicating the chair opposite Brendan as mine. I might have chosen otherwise, but after a small shuffle to reorder the arrangement Emily had wrecked, it was the last open seat.

Three low centerpieces were flanked by a myriad of fresh-baked rolls, each woven into intricate braids or bearing the shape of some sort of flower. When drinks were poured, tentative conversations started around the table, talk of pleasant weather and the new wing on one of the downtown buildings. We were served soups and salads that bore little resemblance to either, and I wondered if they realized this neither honored nor impressed their "prophecy girl." When the salad was removed and a plate of some small not-quite-beige thing that could only be fish was set in front of me, I glanced at the other end of the table.

Brendan, uncharacteristically casual with his shirt sleeves still rolled halfway up his forearms, alternated between small talk and an insincere smile, and surreptitious glances at the girl beside him. Emily picked at what appeared to be leaves and berries sprouting from her entrée, and then sat her fork gently on the side of her plate.

By the time dinner was cleared, conversation had picked up and the guests were getting braver with their topic choices.

"We never imaged you had a sister, Brianna. So unexpected," Kara was saying from the center of the table opposite them. She was the only woman of the Division's eight, and the first to leave Council to join Brendan. I didn't trust her at all.

Brianna made polite small talk, but I was fairly certain she felt the same way.

It had indeed been a surprise to all of us that the heart of the prophecy not only had a sister, but a twin. What was more surprising, however, was that none of their records reflected that detail. There were several theories, the most popular being that the girls' mother had orchestrated the cover-up from the beginning. Knowing what I knew now, I had no doubt.

Talk turned to the troubles of late, barely skirting the chief taboo of the evening: Morgan. Bringing up the name of the man the guest of honor was hiding from would not only be ill-mannered, it would lead to the questions the Division was trying to keep from answering directly. So far, they'd managed to inform Brianna of Morgan's desire for her, his power to sway, and the danger to the rest of us. What they'd been afraid to disclose, however, was the prophecy, and how central she was to their plan.

While Eric and Seth discussed the messes being made by Council, the commonbloods who were being used and then left without cover stories or explanations of any kind, I considered again what Emily's life must have been like, knowing her sister was the chosen and being held responsible for her safekeeping.

A small white plate of custard drizzled with chocolate and caramel pulled me from my thoughts and I glanced down the table at Emily, who finally looked like she'd found something she could eat. She lifted the tiny dessert fork, but stopped short at the turn of conversation.

"Four of them, beaten near death and dumped roadside with no explanation," Seth complained.

She stared across the table at him, her hand dropping slowly to return the utensil.

Eric sat beside Seth, joining in, "We're spending our resources on cleaning up after them. They aren't even adhering to the oldest codes. If we miss something, it will be on the news. The commonbloods..."

Emily's hands went into her lap as they continued. She looked a bit sick.

"... like we have the time and resources to waste on their used commonbloods—"

It was about the sixth time in so many minutes they'd used the label, and Seth's words were cut short as Emily, who was suddenly standing, slammed her fist on the table. "They aren't *commonbloods*, they're people," she said. "Dead. People."

The room fell still. Emily's stare was focused directly on Eric and Seth, so she was unaware that the rest of us could only watch her, could only look on in shock as Brianna's quiet sister transformed from a pretty young brunette into a barely restrained fury. Her eyes were hard, expression not just livid, but outraged, and she was suddenly older. It was as if she'd seen more than any of us in her years, and yet remained shocked at our manners.

Seth had the decency to look shamed at having offended a guest, and Eric inclined his head slightly in apology. The silence became awkward, heavier and heavier, and, eventually, Emily returned to her seat.

But dinner just wasn't the same after that.

15

Sustenance

Dessert sat uneaten on most of our plates, and everyone politely refused coffee. No one was brave enough to attempt conversation again, but had they tried, the look on Brendan's face would have shut them down.

When Brianna finally spoke up, letting on that she was exhausted from the day's excitement, the rest of the table latched on to the pretext and excused themselves for the night.

I saw Brendan whisper something to Brianna, but she merely stared at him for a moment, jaw tight, before leading Emily from the room. When they disappeared through the doorway, I glanced back to Brendan, only to find him giving me a similar look to the one he'd just received.

"What?" I said around a mouthful of bread.

He shook his head and turned for the door Eric and Seth had exited minutes before. I grabbed a few more rolls and wrapped them in a napkin, ignoring the sidelong glances the kitchen staff gave me as they waited to clear the table. I tied the top of the napkin in a quick knot, which, perversely, made me want to whistle the *Andy Griffith Show* theme song for my audience. I hastily made my way from the dining room, smiling as I skipped up the steps two at a time, and nearly ran into Logan around the corner at the top of the stairs.

He raised his brows.

"Logan," I said, grabbing his forearm in Council's traditional greeting.

He didn't hesitate, gripping my own in return. "I was on my way to find you," he said. "I got a message you needed a crew."

"Yes." I glanced down the hallway then, and he tilted his head toward a sunroom on the far end.

I turned to lead the way, Logan wordlessly at my side. He'd been raised by Council law as well, and he had little faith in Brendan's promises. The Division might have been the lesser of two evils, but evil was evil, and neither of us trusted them.

We made our way to the windows, both of us glancing at the shadows reflected against the glass as darkness stole its true purpose. Logan reached into a pocket of his black cargo pants and pulled out a small plastic device to lay on a nearby table.

He pressed a button before turning back to me. "That should do it."

I smiled, imagining how long it would take the security team to figure out they'd been scrambled.

Logan glanced around the room. Neither of us had much love for "the beige house" either. "How long will you stay?"

"Looks like three nights," I said. "There's been a bit of a complication, I'll need to sort it out first."

He nodded. "The girl." He shrugged at my grimace. "Word travels fast. What do you plan to do with her?"

"I don't know." I rubbed a hand over the muscles at my neck, remembering my broken shoulder. "I can't leave her here, but she won't go without Brianna."

He pursed his lips, not wanting to ask his next question. "Can you not *make* her?"

A breath huffed out involuntarily. "Doesn't seem to be the case. Aside from that, however, I don't trust them with her."

"Wait," Logan said, suddenly at attention, "you *can't* make her?"

His surprise had me taken aback, and I struggled to explain why it had made sense to me. "Well, I hit my head." Which was now fully healed and apparently working with everyone else. "And then..." And then what? Logan stared at me. "Her sister is the chosen. We don't know, well, we can't know what should work on them."

Logan waited for something I'd said to make sense. A long moment later, he said, "So we leave her here. With the chosen."

I was shaking my head before he finished. "No. She's too dangerous. She thinks she's meant to protect Brianna and she'll end up doing something stupid." Reckless. Permanent.

"Aern—"

"And I don't trust them. I can't, Logan. I just can't."

He watched me for a long time, my tailored shirt, my messy hair. My tied-up dinner napkin. "All right," he said finally. "Then what do we do with her?"

"I don't know," I answered truthfully. "I don't know yet."

A tiny red light began to flash on the scrambling device. Logan held up his first and second fingers: two minutes.

"We're moving on Morgan," I said. "I can't play cat-and-mouse any longer, he's getting too close."

Logan nodded. "I'll have a team together in two days. We will wait for you at the secondary drop point."

"Thank you, Logan."

He only stared at me. We had known each other our whole lives, fought and played side by side for two decades. Our world had crumbled around us, and yet, even when what I was doing made no sense to him, he trusted in my decision. "Two days," he said.

Two days and it would be either me, or Morgan. The unforeseen, or death.

Logan switched the device off and slid it into his pocket. We turned to stare out the darkened glass until the security team rushed into the room. I couldn't help but notice the corner of his mouth turn up at their urgency.

It had taken Brendan to finally calm things down with the security team. He was highly disappointed in both of us, though he clearly had more pressing issues to resolve and didn't stick around to berate us. Logan left the house after restocking his supplies, and I trudged up the stairs to my room, tied napkin in hand.

It was nearly two a.m. when Emily showed up.

I'd been standing in front of the side table, wondering if I should check on her. The napkin full of bread had been an excuse, I knew, and that knowledge was what had kept me from going. But when I heard soft footfalls outside my door, I knew she was standing there, unable for some reason to bring herself to knock. It was that same magnetic polarity that caused me to open the door.

She stared wordlessly at me from the hallway, barefoot in jeans and a plain cotton tee, completely unprepared to explain her late night visit.

"Couldn't sleep?" I supplied.

She seemed grateful for the excuse, though it was probably true, given that we'd both napped most of the afternoon. I stepped aside to let her in, resisting the urge to glance down the hall. The door clicked shut behind me as I turned to face her, and the sound seemed amplified in the empty room. Emily twisted her hands in front of her stomach.

"Sit," I said, taking the napkin from its place on the side table. She returned obediently to her spot on the bed, completely ignoring the reading chairs on the far wall. I pulled up the lightweight chair that sat beneath the narrow, matte black desk to sit in front of her and untied the knot. When she saw the bread, her unease melted away. I offered the open bundle to her and she pulled a braided roll from the small pile.

She held it in front of her, tearing a section away with one hand, and then stopped. "I'm sorry," she muttered.

"For what?"

She rolled her eyes in a gesture much like the one Brianna had displayed earlier. They were very much alike, she and her sister, but not indistinguishable. Emily's hair was sun-streaked, less orderly. Her eyes were not quite so wide, or at least, I thought, didn't seem so against fuller cheeks and decisive expression.

"It doesn't mean anything," I said. "It's just a little less conspicuous than calling them humans."

She bit her lip, not wanting to ask the obvious question.

I sighed and sat the napkin on the bedside table. "We are all human, Emily. There is very little of that *other* in us now. It's just an expression. Old habits die hard, is all." It wasn't entirely true. Many of the eldest refused to believe we were anything like the humans. But I didn't need to tell her that now.

"Brianna and me," she said, "are we... other?"

"I don't know," I said truthfully. She put down her uneaten bread and I took her hands. "We may never know how you tie into our lines, Emily. Your mother wanted it that way. If she was a prophet, then she had good reason." I stared into her green eyes. "But you have to know, whatever you are, you are special."

"I think that came out way cornier than you meant it," she said. When I didn't respond, she swallowed hard, and pulled her hands free of mine. "I just can't do this," she said. "I can't sit there playing nice while one of them might be the one who wants to kill Brianna."

I sat back in my chair. She was right. But until Morgan was contained, the Division was the only safe place for Brianna. I had to leave her here, but I couldn't expect Emily to abandon her.

"Two days," I said. "Give me two days and you can take Brianna and run." Take Brianna and run? Was I so sure of my failure? So certain of the prophecy?

"What happens in two days?" she asked.

I shook my head. "Eat. We will talk about it later." When I figured it out myself.

Several hours later, we'd fallen back into our former locations on the bed. I couldn't be sure how it had happened exactly, but we both seemed to migrate toward it, that comfort that waited where she lay in my arms and rested her head on my chest. We talked softly of her sister, Emily's stories reinforcing my first impression of the girl.

"What does she think of Brendan?" I asked, certain there was a good story there. If I'd had to describe Brianna before seeing them together, it would have been with words like "meek" and "unassuming," but the way she'd spoken to Brendan had me questioning my assessment. But, in truth, Brendan wasn't exactly himself around her, either. Something about Brianna set his teeth on edge.

Emily laughed and I knew I wasn't the only one to notice. "I suppose she'll let me know when she figures it out," she said. "She knows you don't trust him, but she likes to form her own opinions."

"Fair enough," I said.

"And what does Brendan think of her?" she asked.

I smiled. "He keeps his opinions to himself." I hesitated, remembering his concerns. "Does Brianna have any visitors, anyone bringing her messages?"

She tilted her head up to look at me. "That's what he thinks? That she's got a spy on the inside?"

I shrugged. "I'm not sure what he thinks, but apparently it involves your sister knowing things."

Her head fell back to its earlier position as she stared across the room. "That's just Brianna. She always knows things."

We were quiet for a while, both of us lost in thought, and Emily's gaze fell upon my forearm where it rested on my abdomen. She reached tentatively out to touch the place my scars had been, the once-jagged knife wounds that were now smooth skin. Her index finger rose slightly as her middle finger traced delicately over the skin. Her touch was so light, so perfect as it trailed over me, it became unbearable not to touch her in return. And touching her was so wrong.

I swallowed against a dry throat, shifting slightly beneath her, and brought up the one topic that would keep me from acting. "Is Brianna well?"

Emily's hand froze on my arm, her fingers poised birdlike above my skin, and I wondered what I'd said wrong.

"She looked a little pale earlier," I explained. "If she isn't feeling well, we can help."

I felt Emily's back ease as she released a breath. "Oh, no, she'll be all right. It's just, sometimes she gets like that." She seemed to realize this wasn't answer enough, and added, "When she's tired."

The topic effectively ended our discussion, and we lay silent, Emily's hand still as it lay over my chest. And though neither of us needed to, we slept.

16

A Turn for the Worse

Breakfast was far more private. Brendan had apparently learned his lesson, and only allowed Kara and Seth to join us at the small round table beneath the skylights that surrounded the entrance to the kitchen. When Emily and Brianna arrived, Kara slid fluidly into the seat to Brendan's left, leaving only a free chair between myself and Seth on one side and myself and Kara on the other. Brianna chose Seth's side.

"I trust you all slept well," Kara said, as if we were guests in her house. I pointedly did not look at Emily as she arranged the napkin in her lap, head down. "Of course," Kara continued, "we can make other arrangements if any of you are uncomfortable."

I realized then that she was not implying anything about us, but rather Brianna, whose eyes were shadowed more than usual. I laid a hand over hers. "Are you well, Brianna?"

Her eyes flickered just the tiniest bit, as if the pupils had constricted to pinpoints and then flashed back to normal. I narrowed my gaze on her, but she stared steadily into my eyes, and I decided the reflection of the skylights must have been playing tricks on me. "I'm fine," she said, "only anxious for this to be over."

"Soon," I promised, hating the lie. No matter what happened, Brianna would be forced into a life she couldn't want. Even if, by some miracle, we removed Morgan and Council fell back into order, the Division would come for her. She was the key to the prophecy, and she'd never rest until a path was fulfilled.

I looked up, recognizing that the table had fallen silent, and found them all staring at the two of us, a daughter of great power and second heir to the dragon's name, my hand lying gently over hers. I had the sudden, infuriating sensation of being pushed into something I didn't want, and I had to consciously remove the glower from my face. My hand returned to the silverware, but only as pretense.

Seth attempted small talk with Emily, failed miserably, and then moved on to repeating jokes he'd heard from Logan the night before. But Logan had a dry sense of humor, and generally delivered them in a subtle manner that Seth simply couldn't master. After the first few fell flat, he clicked his tongue and went back to his food. This made Emily smile, though all of his efforts had not, and she finally forked up a large bite of the scrambled egg she'd been picking at.

Brendan looked, if not pleased, at least a bit less annoyed now that she'd apparently decided they were not trying to poison her. Brianna, who had yet to touch her own plate, raised her gaze to the door. It was a full six seconds later before Wesley walked through it.

As he approached Brendan's right side, Wesley locked eyes with Brianna in an all-too-brief instant that would have meant nothing had he not immediately looked down to break their connection as he handed Brendan a report. My eyes narrowed on Brianna, who looked as if she were about to be ill, and then Brendan's fist crashed against the table, sending silverware and dishes to clanging.

He cursed, clenched his jaw tight, and then handed the paper back to Wesley. "Gather a meeting, I'd like some control in how this gets out."

Wesley hurried from the room and Brendan pressed the base of his palm firmly against his forehead before looking up to let us in on the bad news.

"Three different sources are reporting Morgan had a row with a couple senior Council members. After the disagreement, it seems that one of the men walked to the encased display knives and stabbed himself in the chest, directly through his heart." There was a gasp from my right, and Kara covered her mouth with a manicured hand. Brendan's jaw flexed and he swallowed hard. "The other abruptly changed his opinion, and knelt on the ground before Morgan's feet."

"No," Seth said from beside him, "no, it's not possible."

"I might have agreed with you, Seth, if not for their character."

"Who?" I said. "Which ones?"

Brendan sighed. "Caleb and Noah."

"Oh gods." Kara sounded sick. We all knew Caleb and Noah. Neither of them were the sort of man to commit suicide, or kneel down to Morgan.

It was true then. Morgan had figured out a way to use the sway against our own kind. He could control them.

He could control us all.

"Four more of the Council have receded, but at this point I don't know who we can trust," Brendan said. "I'm afraid to bring anyone else to our side if the influence is genuine."

"He has to be stopped," Kara said. "This isn't right. No one should have that power."

Emily huffed quietly beside me at Kara's hypocrisy, but there was no humor in it. This was bad for everyone, but Brianna most of all. Without our immunity, there was no one to keep her safe.

And then a lead weight settled in my stomach. There was no one to keep any of us safe.

"But what about—" Seth started, and then suddenly remembered Brianna beside him and fell dumb.

"We should continue this in the conference room," Brendan said. He glanced at me. "Aern?"

I subtly shook my head. No matter that I'd left Brianna under their protection, no matter that I was staying in their house, I would not join the Division simply because we shared the same enemy. I still had some choice. I wasn't certain exactly what that was at the moment, but there had to be another option.

Kara glared at me openly, but Brendan and Seth didn't take the time to try and convince me. The three of them were gone a moment later, and we sat alone at the small round table, the dragon, the prophecy girl, and her twin.

When Emily realized Brianna was crying, she startled us all by moving. She crossed to Brianna, who'd not made a sound but bore red-rimmed eyes and telltale tracks of a few escaped tears, and led her silently from the table.

I walked to the balcony, and stood unaccompanied for some time before Ellin found me and asked if there was anything I needed. There was. I gave her a list and she nodded before quickly disappearing.

It was Wesley who delivered the disposable phones.

"Is there anything else I can do?" he asked.

I leaned against the balcony railing; the chill wind bit at my exposed skin. Wesley didn't appear to notice the temperature, or my critical gaze.

"Do you have any information that I should know about?"

He went a little pale.

"Because, unlike the others, I have only one goal here. I intend to save Brianna, prophecy or no."

He shook his head in a stuttered nod. "Yes… I mean, no. No there's nothing I haven't reported."

I frowned. "There is something between you and Brianna, Wesley."

A sort of shudder ran through him, and he sputtered out denials so quickly I could only understand every third word.

"Calm down," I said, stepping toward him. "Brianna is not the enemy. If you've been feeding her information—"

"No," he spat. "No, I mean no, sir. I would never… The Division is all I have left. I couldn't—" He was swiftly approaching the risk of hyperventilation.

"Wes, it's okay. I only want you to tell me what it is. If there is something going on, I need to know. For Brianna."

He nodded, gulping air as he did so. I gave him a few minutes to gather himself before trying again.

"What is it then?"

His face had recovered from the pallor, but he unexpectedly colored at the idea of answering. I stared at him, a flash of disbelief. Surely they weren't…

"No!" Wesley cried, seeing my expression, "How could you even… No." He groaned. "Brianna, she's just… she's helping me is all."

Silence hung between us for a moment. "Helping you?"

He shifted his feet, glanced at the lawn. "You know how it is," he muttered, "with Brendan and… before."

I felt my shoulders relax. Whatever Brianna and Wesley were doing, it didn't seem to be dangerous. I waited for the rest of the explanation.

He nervously wrenched a hand over the side of his neck, not wanting to delve into further embarrassment. "She saw the trouble I was having... she saw Brendan and the others, how things were going, and she offered to help. That's all, Mr. Archer, I swear it. I would never tell her—"

I held up a hand to stop him, glancing pointedly at the balcony doors to his back, before carrying on a feigned conversation. "That will work perfectly, Wesley. And thank you for the prompt delivery of these phones. Oh, Ellin." I glanced at her before a cursory nod at Wesley to dismiss him, and though he managed to school his features, his eyes betrayed an eternal gratefulness for the escape.

Ellin handed me a folder. "Mr. Archer," she said in greeting, exhibiting the flawless business manner Brendan expected of all his staff. "If there is anything else I can do for you, please let me know."

"This is sufficient for now, Ellin. Thank you." I slipped the folder under my arm. "But could you have something sent up for Brianna?" She waited. "Hot tea, I think."

Ellin nodded, barely able to maintain her impassive façade at the reference. I winked, certain the whole house was whispering about the state the prophecy girl had their stalwart leader in, and Ellin quickly spun to go. It felt odd to be anything but serious in a moment like this, but it seemed to happen of its own accord these days. I guessed my training was kicking in. If there was anything my father had taught me, it was to be calm in the face of disaster. Excitement spread like fire, and in the end someone always got burned.

Ellin had closed the balcony doors behind her, but both of us knew I didn't have any real privacy. Not that it mattered; if my suspicions were correct, there would be no need of it. I pocketed one of the phones, flipped the other open.

When I dialed Avery, I had some hope. But there was nothing, not so much as a "this line has been disconnected" message on the other end. By the time I tried Nathan, I knew I wouldn't be able to reach any of them. Morgan had managed to cut me off from all of those loyal to Council traditions, all those who might have been a help. I snapped the card from the back of the disposable phone and tossed it.

I leaned against the rail to page through the reports Ellin had given me. As I read the final page, I sighed. From the looks of things, the flicker of unrest was the least of our problems. We were about to walk into the flames of hell.

17

IRRESISTIBLE FORCES

As I walked through the halls, I overheard several small arguments and agitated conversations regarding what was to be done about Morgan and the Council. Apparently the meeting had broken up, and Brendan hadn't been able to satisfy his followers with whatever mode of action, or inaction, he'd decided on. I hoped none of them were brave enough to attempt it on their own, and then internally flinched at the idea of my own intentions. Two days, and I still didn't have a plan.

I knew I could get close to Morgan, there was no question of that. He would put on a show for what was left of Council, place his arrogant younger brother on display while he spouted quotes like "see how the mighty have fallen." But Morgan had never truly underestimated me. In all the years he treated me as his subordinate, he'd never trusted that I was. He simply wanted to keep me in check, keep up the pretense and watch my every move. I tried not to think of what he might have done to the others. If he could bring a man to stab himself in the heart over a disagreement, he would surely have acted against those who'd openly supported me, those who had wanted me to take his place.

I turned the corner to the hall our rooms were on and froze.

Emily stood in the center of the corridor, staring up at Eric. The moment lasted an eternity, my chest tight as I took in the scene. Eric, of the Division, never a member of Council and never trusted, was inches from Emily, his hand resting on her arm—the hand that he needed to work his sway, the hand he'd used to manipulate human women, the hand that could tear her mind apart.

My muscles unfroze and I was running for him before my mind could process anything further. He was touching her. He was touching Emily.

He only had time to turn his head before I slammed into him. The two of us landed several feet from where he'd stood, and I had his head in a lock hold before he realized he'd been attacked. But Eric was big and solid, and one of the best fighters among the Division. He pressed a foot against the corridor wall and pushed, using his mass to roll us both. I tightened my grip, cutting off his air supply, and he threw an elbow into my ribs and then rolled backward in an attempt to flip out of the hold.

It didn't work and he flailed, halfway over, and then came down hard before spinning sideways and using the wall to roll us again. When he got his feet, he raised us both, and slammed me into the wall where I clung behind him. I dropped the hold and drew back to strike him when Brendan burst out the door beside me and grabbed my arm. Suddenly he and Seth and Kara were struggling to separate us and yelling profanities.

The lot of us fell silent when Brianna stepped into the hall.

"I'm sorry," Brendan said after a moment. He glared at me. "I don't know what's gotten into him."

"He's only protecting us," Brianna replied, but her words were for me, not Brendan.

And then I realized they'd all come out of Brianna's room.

"You aren't in danger here," Brendan said, looking at first to Emily and then Brianna. "Neither of you."

His glare met Eric then, and it was clear he wasn't included in the promise of safety.

Eric wiped his mouth. "I was apologizing, that's all." He looked at me, started to say more, and then pushed past all of us to leave.

Kara scowled at me again, crossed her arms and followed Eric's lead.

"We'll talk more later," Brendan told Brianna, and then shook his head one final time before he and Seth went as well.

I shrugged to straighten my shirt, and then crossed to Emily, who stood silent, as if watching the scene replay before her. I grabbed her, a hand on each side of her head, and her eyes went wide as I stared into them, searching. I didn't know what I expected to find, some telltale sign, some revealing feature that said she'd been hurt, but I couldn't stop looking.

"Aern," Brianna said from beside us. "She's fine." She placed a gentle hand on my arm. "I'm sorry I left her alone."

My shoulders sagged at her words, and I loosened the grip I had on Emily.

"Come," Brianna said, "we'll have some tea."

In the end, I had begged off the invitation. In a day and a half, I would be meeting Logan and the others to go after Morgan. I had to be prepared.

Though I hadn't mentioned my plans to anyone aside from Logan, Brianna had said she understood. She had told me to rest and the answers would come. I didn't suppose it was any real secret that Morgan had to be stopped, or that I was a likely candidate to take action, but that didn't keep Brendan's words from returning. *She knows too much.*

I shook my head and went back to the reports in front of me. None of it mattered if I didn't find a way to stop Morgan.

He'd managed to split us off from everyone who remained associated with Council. He'd recruited youth, he'd threatened elders, he'd made them take sides. And now there was nothing left to salvage.

Even if it wasn't true, even if Morgan didn't have the ability to sway our own kind, he'd succeeded in tearing apart the brotherhood among Council. He'd destroyed all trust. He'd forced us to war with our own kind. Men had died, and this was only the beginning.

I read through page after page of reports from the Division's men. Warehouse purchases, missing person reports, human profiles, burned buildings, money transfers. Morgan was so thick into so many varied affairs, it was hard to see any pattern to his dealings. But one factor was prominent across the board: acquisition. He was gathering. Weapons. Buildings. Businesses.

People.

He had amassed untold numbers, our kind and commonblood. He was building an army. He would be unstoppable.

The Division could not handle a war of so many without resorting to Morgan's methods. And even if they stooped to his level, the battle couldn't be won by humans. It wouldn't be over until our kind was wiped out on one side or the other. And there would be none of us left, the prophecy had made that clear. The prophecy had given only two outcomes. Both involved destruction, but there was only one choice that didn't end in Armageddon. There was only one option to save us all.

Page after page, report after report, nothing I could see would hold up to Morgan. Whether he truly held sway against our own kind or not, nothing short of the chance Division had given me would do it. And it was the one thing I wasn't sure I could do.

"Can I help?"

Emily's words startled me and I looked up, surprised to find her standing in the doorway of the library. How long had she been there?

She took a few tentative steps forward. "I need something to do," she said, glancing over her shoulder. "I can't just sit here, when they might be... when Brianna..."

I closed the folder on the desk in front of me. "I understand." I was feeling helpless, too. "I was only going through some financials, some of the intel they've gathered on Morgan's doings."

She nodded, coming closer. "Any luck?"

She wasn't going to come right out and ask me what we planned to do. She knew I couldn't tell her, even if I'd wanted to. And, honestly, I had no idea what Brendan's plans were.

"There's a lot to go through," I offered. "You're welcome to join me."

She let out a relieved breath and sat opposite me in a large brocade reading chair, the desk between us. "Great. Where do I start?"

I passed a folder over, the contents innocuous enough even if it was fifty pages of small print. "We're looking for anything suspicious, anything that might indicate a strike point or strategy."

She stared up at me. "You mean you think he's going to attack you."

"The Division," I corrected. "Morgan has a personal vendetta against me, but the Division is his only true adversary. The one group with the knowledge of his legitimacy and the means to stop him." The one group that would challenge his rule.

Her brows drew together, and I thought she meant to say something, but she nodded slowly and looked down at the folder in her lap. I watched her as she settled in to her task, the truth in my words falling away from the rest in my mind.

No one else did understand the threat. No one but Council and the Division understood the importance of this decision. Council had already fallen to Morgan. I didn't think I had ever truly believed it possible, in all the years I'd been taught the prophecy. How could Council, the entity that raised me, the being that embodied our entire history, fall apart? But it had. It had been taken down. And the Division was next.

I had to do something, I knew that. But even if I managed to reach Morgan, if I somehow overtook him, tricked him, stabbed him in the heart the first instant I came close enough, nothing would be solved. The Council was in ruin, there would be no reconciliation between the lines, and all that awaited was the end of days.

But Morgan did have sway against his own. And if I reached him, he could turn me. Brendan's pleading tore at me. *You are our only chance.*

So that was it, then. It was the union or nothing. It didn't matter that I didn't want reign over Council, over all our kind. It was the only way.

My eyes involuntarily found Emily, feet propped on the desk as she turned page after page and scanned through the addresses. It had always seemed like the last option, the final, never-to-be-used backup plan, but deep down I didn't doubt I would have surrendered to the Division and created the union with Brianna all along if I'd needed to. If it meant saving the world. But now, watching Emily, it seemed like more of a sacrifice than I remembered.

I would be bound to Brianna.

But it wouldn't be long, would it? In two days, I was likely to die at the hands of Morgan. I might save the others, I might give them all a chance, but there wasn't any guarantee I would make it. There was no way to know if Morgan would use his sway to turn me against those I'd meant to protect in some sick notion of rightfulness.

There wasn't a surety of anything.

It was the best I could do, though. The best chance at keeping them both from harm.

Emily reclined in the chair, and I couldn't help but think

of the first night I'd held her in my arms. This time, I didn't stare at my boots. I let my eyes roam over her, memorizing every part, lingering on the line of her neck, the curve of her lips. I could still see the way the sunrise colored her face through the hotel window, could still recall the sweet scent of her shampoo.

A horrified, "No," slipped from Emily's lips and then her feet fell from the desk to land hard on the floor beneath her. She was suddenly standing, staring at me. Terrified.

"What is it?" I asked, around the desk before I'd had time to process her reaction.

The folder fell away, and only the stack of papers remained in her hand, thirty or so pages back.

"Emily, what?" I begged.

Her eyes fell to the paper, her other hand pointing to a small, insignificant line. It was an address, a city southwest of here. I didn't understand the connection.

"My mother," she whispered. "Oh no, no, no—"

I grabbed her arms, gave her a firm shake to make her look at me.

"This address, this is where we lived..." She looked sick. "When my mother was taken."

18

Revelations

I put a hand on a gasping Emily's waist to usher her to my room. I had a feeling no one from the Division needed to hear our conversation. We were no more than through the door when she turned on me.

"Where did you get this?"

I watched her, not the stack of papers in her hand violently shaking in my direction. "We—" I stopped myself. "The Division has information-gatherers. Spies."

She threw the stack to the floor, where it landed soundlessly on plush beige carpeting. "And they found them with Council. Do you know what that means? Do you?"

I stared at her. I had a feeling my idea of what it meant

— 161 —

and her idea of what it meant were on two different planes.

She took a step toward me, a threat in her voice. "It means *your* people did this, Aern. Not the Division. Council, the ones we're supposed to trust."

My instincts told me to back slowly away, but my mouth had other ideas. "You know they aren't to be trusted now. You heard the report. Morgan has figured out a way to sway our own kind—"

"No," Emily said. "Not *now*. This isn't a new report. My mother, *our* mother, was taken before Morgan got this sway—"

Emily suddenly grabbed her middle as if she'd been punched in the gut. "Oh no," she groaned, shaking her head.

I reached for her and she put up a hand between us. "No. No, Aern, I… Oh no."

"For the last time, what is it?" I was hovering over her where she hunched forward, my hands helplessly waiting.

"Nothing," she said, waving the hand she'd held up. "Nothing, I, I have to…"

Her words were lost to me as she leaned over to pick up the papers. She was wearing clothes Brianna had gotten for her, clothes I presumed were Emily's usual style, and the hem of the fitted Henley that had rested at her waist rode up to reveal the skin of her lower back.

"Christ," I said. "Oh, Christ."

Emily's head turned to find me, momentarily distracted from her own agitation. She opened her mouth to ask "What?"

and then her eyes, her wide, sea-glass-green eyes, followed mine and she realized what I'd seen.

My stomach turned. "Tell me it's only a tattoo."

She straightened, face pale despite having just righted herself.

I stepped closer. "Emily, tell me. Tell me you got a tattoo. Tell me you stayed out late, fell in with the wrong crowd, made some bad decisions, tell me you woke up with this and have no idea how it got there."

Her cheeks flushed. "Ancient blood rite symbols? I don't think so, Aern."

I could see that she was embarrassed at my reaction, but I couldn't stop myself. I grabbed her waist, spun her around, and moved her shirt aside to bare the top of an inked design on her lower left side.

She glanced back at me over her shoulder. "It's not, it wasn't like that, Aern. My mother. She… I told you about her. You know." She was mortified now, having to explain her crazy mother's ideas. "She did it when I was too young to argue with her."

But her mother wasn't crazy. She was a prophet. I swallowed hard before running my thumb over the design.

The words were stuck in my throat, choking me. All of it, the whole ordeal would have spilled out, but something like a single weak cough was all I could manage.

Emily turned slowly toward me, the gravity of my reaction sinking in. This wasn't about some tattoo. This was something else. Something about the ancient symbols. Something about Brianna. "What?" she whispered, half afraid to find out more.

My hands were still at her hips, frozen there, my thumbs resting on the bare skin above her jeans. The bare skin of the chosen.

I fell to my knees in front of her, pulling her down to face me. Her mouth hung slightly open, unsure whether to brace for hurt or anger or fear. I had trusted my room was secure. I had trusted we had privacy. I'd said anything I'd needed to say here freely, but not this. Not these words.

My right hand freed her waist to curve gently around the base of her neck. I pulled her in, the image of those same symbols carved into Brianna's wrists clear in my mind as I pressed my cheek to Emily's and whispered the words that could never be taken back. The words that would ruin her.

"Brianna is a decoy."

Emily stiffened under my hand, but I held her there, my lips moving swiftly, my voice all but silent.

"Your mother hid your mark. You were born with the symbol, I can feel it on your skin. The tattoo is only a cover. Brianna's are as well. She put them on the inside of her wrists so they would find them. So they would stop looking before they came to you. There's a curve beneath the symbol of the serpent that spirals up and right. She traced the ink to the left and down. It's a small change, but that's all she needed. She marked you as merely Brianna's blood, but she knew they'd find her first. She knew Brianna would be their target."

The hands Emily had braced against my arms curled tighter as we stayed there. When I'd said all I could say, my head fell forward, resting an inch above her shoulder. Not touching, not now.

Everything had changed. In one instant, the constant we'd lived with our entire lives was gone, swept from beneath us in a heartbeat. It was Emily. *Emily*.

A long moment passed before I noticed her mouth moving silently beside me. I'd been lost in my own revelations, been shifting my own realities. I carefully eased my head back to see her, and caught the forms of several ancient words. Another prophecy.

She was repeating back her mother's teachings, aligning them to her situation. Finding her truth.

Her lips stilled and she looked at me. But she didn't see me. Her green eyes were hollow, a vacant stare from someone lost and mislead.

"I need to see Brianna," she whispered, her voice hoarse.

I nodded, helped her to her feet. There was nothing I could say. Nothing to be done. This was a blow that could not be softened. This one shouldn't be eased.

19

SECRETS

Brianna was waiting for us. She stepped aside the open doorway as we brushed past, and brusquely latched the door behind us when we entered the small sitting area outside her bedroom.

Emily spun, the tension that vibrated through her visible on every feature, and Brianna gestured for us to sit. "The room is secure, we can say whatever needs saying."

Neither of us sat.

When Emily finally let loose, it became very clear that she had suspected, and suspected correctly, that Brianna had known all along.

Brianna's voice was steady. "I will explain, just please—"

She moved toward Emily, hand outstretched, and I found myself shifting from foot to foot, hand running over my jaw. How exactly did one handle a girl fight?

"No," Emily shot out, "don't touch me. You're not going to take this from me. Not this time."

My fidgeting ceased.

"I wasn't," Brianna said. "I wouldn't. But please, just sit down and let me say what I need to say."

Something in Brianna's subdued tone wasn't right. Something about Emily's words.

Emily chewed her lip. "Say it. Say it, then. Make it all right that you both lied to me my whole life, Brianna."

Brianna waited, and Emily finally dropped onto a chair, but she stayed forward, elbows posted taut above her knees.

"You know why I couldn't tell you," Brianna said. "She made me keep it from you. To make you safe."

As Brianna laid out the explanations to her sister, the reality of our situation came crashing down. Emily was the chosen. Not Brianna. Emily, who'd followed me to Morgan's warehouse, who'd hunted me down for stealing her sister. Emily, who was only here because of us.

I turned away from them, facing nothing in that windowless room, and wiped the dampness from my palms. I'd brought her here. She was safe, no one had even known she existed, and I'd brought her among us, thrust her into the middle of our war, and nearly gotten her killed in the process. I could see the car again, smashing into brick just shy of her legs as she ran down the alleyway. I could see her sneaker slipping from the iron railing ten stories up the side of a building. I could see her now, in the hands of the Division. The Division her mother had always warned her would be the death of Brianna…

I was suddenly moving, leaving the room without so much as a word to either of them.

The chaos of my thoughts had aligned, given me a purpose. I had made it to the library, was sifting through papers, when Brendan's voice cut through my resolve.

"Looking for something particular?"

My hand stilled. I took a steadying breath before I glanced up, the picture of ease. "Just hoping we missed something." I closed the folder in front of me. "What brings you out this evening?"

Brendan's chin tilted down but his eyes never left me. "We need to talk, Aern."

"Isn't that what we're doing?"

He crossed his arms loosely in front of his chest. "Word spread about what happened with Eric this morning."

I stiffened despite myself.

"There've been whispers," Brendan said casually, as if it weren't a warning.

"I know how you hate whispers."

Brendan's mouth moved, but it wasn't exactly a smile. "They're saying I should keep the two of you apart," he said. "They think maybe she's the reason you're refusing the union."

He was wrong. So, so wrong.

Brendan's eyes shifted in a "well?" gesture. "Don't be absurd," I said, glancing down to arrange the papers lying over the desk.

Brendan stepped forward. "I don't have an answer for them, Aern. Because, by all accounts, you are too close to the girl." When I didn't respond, he shifted uncomfortably, lowered his voice. "I've seen the way you look at her. She matters to you."

The last folder slammed a little harder than I intended onto the stack. "So they would abandon her to Morgan then? To keep her away from me?"

Brendan's brows rose.

I sighed. "Of course she matters. She's Brianna's sister. She should matter to all of them." I put the folders under my arm and stepped around the desk. "She's the only thing Brianna has left. Morgan would use her like he used Aiden."

It was a low blow, I knew. But there was no way I was backing down now, not after what I'd learned.

"Aiden is the reason I'm here," Brendan said.

"And Brianna is the reason I am," I said on my way past him toward the door.

He didn't stop me, but Kara had been listening from the hallway. She spun to follow me, the pound of her heels punctuating her angry whispers. "How could you? How dare you? I can't even—" She picked up her stride, rushing to overtake mine. "Aern. Look at me."

I glanced at her, not bothering to slow my pace.

"His brother? After all that, you would bring up his brother?"

I did stop then. In heels, she was nearly as tall as I, and her momentum left us too close. "Maybe that's what he needs to be reminded of, Kara. Maybe that's what you all need to be reminded of, the reason we're here. The reason he broke from Morgan. This isn't a game." I leaned toward her, my voice low. "He's a monster. A killer. I've seen it with my own eyes, and there is no one to stop him but me. His blood. *His brother.*"

She backed off, breathless and speechless.

"I will do what I have to to save us. You can tell them that."

Her face fell and she raised a hand, readying her apology, but I waved it off.

She nodded, shamefaced, and turned to go, but I stopped her. "Kara?" She glanced over her shoulder. "Tell them anyone who touches her dies."

I didn't wait for her reaction, but I knew she understood. Emily was off limits, or their savior was gone.

As I sat alone in my room, Brendan's constant warnings swam through my head. *It needs to be now. You are our only chance. You know what needs to be done.*

I could understand him, could understand all of them. I felt the urgency. I knew the prophecy. But I hadn't acted. Something, all along, something had held me back.

And now, I had a secret. Only three of us knew the truth about the chosen. Only one of us knew the rest. I would have to tell Emily the reason Morgan wanted Brianna. I would have to tell her his intentions.

Or I would have to meet Logan and the others in little more than a day, and take care of Morgan forever.

My door swung open and Emily stepped in, hair pulled back, white Henley and jeans, as if she were headed to a baseball game, not the girl who held the fate of the world. I glanced at the door and she turned to close it behind her, sliding the deadbolt home before pacing the center of the room.

Gods, she was beautiful. Even frustrated and trapped and alone. And she was going to hate us for what we'd kept from her.

She chewed her thumbnail until the realization of what she was doing sank in, and then she dropped it, tracing a finger over the end before looking at me.

"She was keeping it from me," she said. "All these years."

My mouth pulled tight in one of those sympathetic, "I'm not sure what to say" gestures.

"And do you know what the worst part is?" she continued. "Do you?"

I remained silent, because I was pretty sure it was a rhetorical question. And because I was pretty sure you should never offer your opinion to an angry woman.

She flopped down on the bed beside me, arms falling lifelessly to the sides. "The worst part is that I can't even be mad at her. I can't even hate them for it because I was doing the same thing. My mother played us both, and neither of us were willing to admit it."

She lay there for a long while, finally glancing over at where I sat, waiting for some kind of response.

I ran a hand over my jeans, trying tenuously for some sort of comforting words, all the while certain this conversation would come back to bite me in the ass when she found out the secrets I'd been keeping. "You know, your mother *was* a prophet." I shifted toward her. "I'm sure she would have had good reason to lead you both as such."

Her eyes went to the ceiling and she stretched an arm over her head. I looked away, searching for anything else to focus on.

"I know," she murmured. "I know."

We sat wordlessly for ten minutes, and I nearly told her about Morgan, about the prophecy, at least as many times. I'd finally decided to get it over with when she slid the toe of one shoe under the heel of the other and kicked off her right sneaker. The other one followed, and I looked back in time to see her slide toward me, push me backward and lean into my chest.

"It feels like this is the only place I have anymore," she whispered, and the words were so low I had to strain to hear them. I was certain she'd feel the tension in my chest, though, the way my heart rate changed, and know I was hiding something.

Her fingers curled to trace small circles on my tee shirt over my breastbone.

My right hand reached over and grabbed her wrist, gently but in earnest. I had to tell her. I had to tell her now.

She looked up at me, not taking her cheek from its place.

How had things gone so far off track? It was only a night ago we'd lain like this talking of her sister. When Emily's biggest worry was her mother's warning of the Division. And the thought stopped me.

Something was wrong. Their mother had known, she'd hidden Emily and used Brianna as a distraction. So why was the prophecy so important, why did she caution her against the Division more than any other danger?

"What is it?" Emily asked.

I leaned forward, keeping her close as we sat up together. "The prophecy," I said, "the one about the Taken, the Division."

Her expression unclouded, suddenly aware of my concern.

"Tell me."

She nodded. "I always had trouble remembering... It was, 'the Taken will die at the hands...' no, wait."

"In the old language," I said. "Tell me how she told you."

And she did. And then she was gasping and grappling for her footing as I pulled her off the bed.

"What are you doing?"

"We should go," I said. "Now."

She bent to grab her shoes, following as I dragged her behind me to gather my own things. "Why, Aern? What did it say?"

"It doesn't mean what you think, Emily. It means we should leave. It means you were right, we should never have come here."

She yanked her arm hard to bring me around to face her, jaw tight. It was evident from her stance she didn't intend to move until I'd explained further.

"It doesn't mean she will die at the hands of the Division. It says she will die *in* Division's hands."

She waited.

"'As the prophet is revealed, so die the others.'"

Emily's face went pale. She'd heard the words before, she knew I was right. She was sick, and I could only imagine her thoughts centered on what was about to happen, what it was probably too late to stop. What she could have prevented if she'd believed her mother, if she'd acted on her gut, if she'd only done one thing differently. And then I wondered if they were her worries or my own.

"I should have listened to you," I said. "I should have known."

She swallowed hard, and then moved to open the door so we could find Brianna.

20

ALL HELL

We stepped into the hallway to find Brianna and Brendan running toward us.

"The hall," Brendan called, and I knew what he meant, turning with Emily to reach the safe room they'd dubbed the hall before it was too late.

She didn't question me, only ran alongside until the thin red line of flashers lit up the corridor. Her hand squeezed tight in mine and I glanced at her, not surprised by the 'it's too late' expression. I tightened my grip on her and pressed against the wall to check the corner to the next hall. I felt Brendan and Brianna behind us, but could hear no others when we crossed to the entrance and punched in the code.

In a matter of seconds, we'd made it to this place, and already I'd heard the first shots from the floor below.

"There," Brendan said, pushing us across the room to a dark-paneled wall. He ripped the painting from its hook and threw it aside, revealing another keypad, another passcode. "Inside," he demanded as soon as the panel started shifting.

We were in a smaller chamber lit only by security lights, a narrow passage to the left and a narrow passage straight ahead, both of which must have been built between the walls of the other rooms.

"We have to split up," Brianna said as she shoved a parcel into Emily's hands. "They're coming for us." She indicated herself and Brendan and I realized what she'd said was true. They would be after Brianna. Not Emily.

Brendan stepped forward. "The north passage takes you down to the edge of the yard. I've got armed men there, we can all go—"

"No," Brianna said. "You and I will go that way. Aern will take Emily through the other passage, by the sheds."

Brendan's eyes went tight. She knew too much.

"This is the only way," Brianna said to no one but Emily, and her hand rested over her sister's as she spoke.

"Wait," I said, shouldering them apart, but not entirely sure why.

Emily blinked.

"Go," Brianna whispered to me. "Wesley will be waiting for you." The certainty in her gaze might have convinced me eventually, but the dull echo of gunfire through the reinforced walls did the trick quick enough.

Emily pressed the black twill-wrapped package against her chest and gave Brianna one last look.

"I had Brendan get them for you," Brianna said. "Use them prudently." She placed her hands over Emily's where they clutched the package and pushed.

"Wait," Emily said, "there's something I have to tell you. I forgot." Her eyes flicked to Brendan, back to Brianna and I somehow knew what she was referring to. I remembered the moments before I'd seen her mark, when she'd been curled over her stomach. She'd had a revelation, what was it, what had she been saying…

"It's all right," Brianna said.

"No," Emily insisted. "No more secrets. It was her, Brianna, he took her and she—"

"I know." The room went still as Brianna confessed. Emily's mouth opened, but no words came.

Brianna sighed. "I'm sorry, Emily. I know. I've known all along."

The pain that twisted Emily's features was cutting. "Then…" She stopped, stumbling for words. "But…" And then, almost desperate, "*Why?*"

Brianna's eyes held Emily's when she answered. "Because I am a prophet. I was born with our mother's gifts."

A long, unspoken message passed between the sisters. They stood before each other, a mirror's reflection by all appearances, alike in body and blood, but they couldn't have been more different.

"It's coming," Brianna whispered. Emily took a deep breath and nodded.

And then a blast sounded in the room outside the chamber and Brendan yelled, "Go!" before pulling Brianna down the north passage. Suddenly, Emily and I were running in the opposite direction. The passage was narrow, my shoulders brushed the wall as I ran. I could hear Emily behind me, feet padding lightly on the bare floor. There were stairs, and then a hard right turn, a low corridor, and then a left, and we were standing in a small alcove beneath a single overhead hatch door.

I looked back at Emily to be certain she was ready. She was bending over, strapping something to her leg. When she straightened, I saw what Brianna had given her, as the last of a set remained at the ready in her hand.

Knives. Brianna's gift had been, from what I gathered, at least three handcrafted fighting knives. I winced when the realization came, when Brianna's words registered with her warning. Her prophecy.

Emily nodded, as if she'd missed my reaction and was merely answering my inquiry on whether she was ready. But before either of us could start the climb, the hatch shifted, and we ducked away, though there was no place to hide in the tiny recess. Fortunately, it was Wesley's copper hair that popped into view.

"Finally," he gasped. "What took you guys so long?"

"Are you clear?" I asked.

He nodded. "Yeah, but the grounds are crawling with Morgan's men, you've got to hurry."

He reached an arm down and I lifted Emily by the waist to him, my hand grazing the strap for the third knife that rested behind her back. She kicked off the top rung of the ladder and disappeared through the opening. It only took a moment before I was climbing out behind her.

"We've got to go now," Wesley explained as we all crouched beneath one of the shed's windows. "Brianna said it would only get worse the longer we waited."

My eyes narrowed on him.

He shook his head. "It's not like that, Aern. She has a gift."

Emily stiffened beside me.

"She helped me," Wesley said, "because she needed me to help you."

"What can you do?" Emily asked. "Because if Brianna said run, and we're not running, then you'd better have something damned fancy hiding up your sleeves."

I was taken aback by her response, but Wesley only reacted. "Right." He shoved a crate aside on the back wall. "There's an opening here, run due south, I'll cover you until you reach the trees."

I stared at him.

"Go," he said. "For the chosen. For all of us."

Emily spared me a brief glance before shoving through the door at a full run.

The lawn was crowded with running, fighting, screaming men. Commonblood, Council, Division. Everywhere. We were less than two yards from the shed when the report from Wesley's rifle echoed off the woods. He would pick off any who targeted us, and in the mayhem, that seemed to be all of them.

Emily flinched at each crack of rifle, each boom of .45, but she didn't slow. We were six yards from the trees now. Five. A large man in black got too close before I could decipher which side he was on and I shouldered into him low and hard, and then spun away before I lost sight of Emily. He fell to the grass behind us as a bullet ripped through his shoulder. Three yards. Two. Emily ducked aside as bark splintered off the tree she headed toward, and gunfire erupted again, peppering both our escape and our attacker. Metal ricocheted off the trees, landing a sharp fragment into the meat of my shoulder, and I threw an arm over her as we adjusted course. But they weren't targeting her.

A round clipped my thigh, but adrenaline kept me going. They were trying to slow me down, incapacitate me. Morgan must have given the order I wasn't to be killed. Not yet. I pushed Emily forward as I struggled to overcome the hitch in my stride. They were gaining ground. There were too many of them.

Emily grabbed my shirt and yanked me into the trees with her, and I realized I'd been lagging. She dodged left around a tall oak and then right to pass another. My shoulder brushed the second tree and I stumbled before we reached the underbrush.

"Aern," she hissed, grabbing at me again. Shots fired from in front of us now, and she hunched forward as she pulled me right and through a patch of saplings.

The trees were crawling with men. Morgan's men. There was no question this time who was winning, who was after us.

"There," I said, disturbed by the distant quality of my own voice.

She followed my direction, heading toward a grove of fir trees. The snap and shuffle of the forest floor behind us made it clear there were not just trained men after us. They could make a mistake. They could fire on Emily to stop me. They could take out the chosen.

"Aern!" Emily screamed as I fell behind her. We'd been running, and I realized belatedly that I'd not loosened my grip on her when I'd gone down, that I'd taken her with me. "What is wrong with you?" she gasped. She rolled me to my side, her hands frantically hovering over me, searching for a gunshot wound.

I could feel the blood soaking my leg, but she didn't pause there, instead staring open-mouthed at the thin sliver of metal protruding from the front curve of my shoulder. I forced my gaze to follow hers, but my neck didn't seem to be connected properly.

Emily clenched her teeth and winced as she wrenched the metal from deep within the muscle. When she held it in front of my face, I could see the small feathered tip of a poisonous dart. By the time my brain processed what was happening, my body had begun clearing the toxins from my system. But it wasn't fast enough.

Emily flinched as another shot landed too close beside us.

"Go," I said. "There's a hatch beneath the trees. Hide there. Run."

"What?" she hissed. "Aern—"

"Go, Emily. They don't know." The feeling returned to my arms then, though my fingers still tingled, and I pressed myself up. They were closing in, taking their time. They thought they had us pinned down. Thought we had no place to go.

"They're shooting at you," she said.

"I know." I worked my neck, testing my recovery. "Me. Not you."

She understood, but she couldn't seem to leave, despite the soldiers amassing in the forest around us.

I stood then, pulling her up to stand close before me. A strange, burning numbness prickled my legs. I still couldn't feel the gunshot wound in my thigh. "I'll run with you to the third maple tree." She listened to my instructions, her eyes never straying from mine, never allowing anyone watching to guess the route I was laying out. "… there is a built-in keypad on the wall, the others will find you by morning…"

She let me finish before she spoke again, barely above a whisper. "But—"

I stopped her and she swallowed hard. She thought I was

sacrificing myself for her, she thought they would gun me down the moment they had a clear shot, that I would die on the forest floor beneath us.

"They won't do it, Emily. Morgan has given them orders. I'm to be captured."

It wasn't a lie. They wouldn't kill me here. They would take me in, because he would want the honor.

She stared up at me, not entirely convinced.

"I swear to you, Emily, I will not die here."

I pushed down the guilt at misleading her. She had to stay safe. She was the chosen. She had to live.

"Put your hands over your heads," a voice called from the other side of a clearing. "Turn slowly toward the sound of my voice."

Emily's eyes glistened, but she never looked away from me.

A wave of dizziness made my head spin. I had to convince her, she had to go. "You first," I said. "I'll be right behind you until the third maple. It's the only way, Emily. The only way."

I'd used Brianna's words, and it seemed to strengthen her resolve, or at least remind her of the importance of staying alive. Remind her of the prophecy. After a long moment, her expression changed, and she gave the slightest nod.

The frontline moved closer. We stared into one another's eyes, strengthening our courage.

"Okay," she breathed. "Okay."

The pain in her words did something to me, and I was suddenly reaching for her. My hands braced her there as I pressed my forehead to hers and held her. Just long enough for a silent promise. I would come back to her.

I *had* to come back to her.

21

Confessions

It hadn't been my intention to actually get shot. I'd planned to distract the gunmen, to give Emily a chance to make it to safety, then to fall as soon as she'd cleared the outer branches of the copse of fir trees and let them think they had me. But Morgan's order must have been a little looser than I'd estimated, because as soon as we'd started to run, they opened fire.

Had I not been face down in dirt and leaves writhing in agony, I might have appreciated the fact that my plan had actually worked. Because I'd told Emily I was going to go down when the first warning shots fired, she didn't look back. She thought I had played my part, and she was upholding her end of the bargain. She was running for safety.

Another report sounded in her general direction and I coughed blood and leaf bits into the dirt as I struggled to lift my head.

"Down!" a voice yelled from behind me. "Stay down!"

A heavy boot smashed into my side once, twice. "Turn him," someone ordered, "keep your eyes on his hands."

Another boot kicked against my hip, rolling me to land on my back, though an arm was trapped beneath me. I could only feel the pressure now, the cool air rushing over my skin, the warm wetness of the leaves below me. With immense effort, I managed to twist my chin to see the direction she should have been. I held my breath, closed one eye, concentrated hard on bringing her into focus.

There was shouting, the rush of boots on underbrush. I closed both eyes. Took a deep breath.

"Don't move!" the voice beside me yelled again. There was some fumbling around my ankles. And then the vague notion I'd been shot in the side. And there was darkness. I had to focus. She had to make it. I had to see her make it.

I opened my eyes and found Emily. My chest tightened. The white Henley, her honeyed hair. The last flash of the bottom of her sneakers as she crashed through the thick green branches to refuge. Her nearest pursuer was too far, they'd never find her, they'd never have her. I felt my mouth pull back into a smile as I slipped into the darkness of oblivion.

I wasn't sure how long I'd slept, but it hadn't been long enough.

"Again," a harsh voice yelled as icy water was thrown into my face.

A tearing, awful pain shot through my side as my body reacted to the shock, but my mind hadn't caught up with what was happening. I couldn't see where I was, didn't know anything but that it was too bright, too loud, too *real*.

"Clean up his face, I don't want it to look like a butcher's shop here."

I attempted to lift my head, but it only bobbed before my chin fell back against my chest. A towel was pressed to my cheek, roughly brushing away what blood the water hadn't. It smelled of bleach and disinfectant, the too-clean scent of hospital linen. But this wasn't a clinic.

"Could be the poison, sir," a different voice offered, this one closer than the first.

"Don't be a fool," the first voice said. "Give him one hour of sleep and he'll be healing every single wound you've handed him."

My brain made the connection then, put a face to the voice.

But before my eyes would open, he was closer, drawing out the words as he spoke in my ear. "He's an Archer. He has the power of the blood."

Morgan.

His hand fisted into my hair as he jerked my head up to face him. "Wake, brother. We've got plans for you."

I spat blindly in his direction.

"Open your eyes," he said in a tone so lethal it silenced the rest of the room.

Surprisingly, I did open them this time, though the chamber swam heavily. Morgan yanked my head again and my gaze finally settled on him.

"There, was that so difficult?"

He looked different somehow, the hard lines of his face sharper, the angry set of his jaw tighter. I studied his face, but all trace of boyishness was gone. There didn't seem to be any chance of his trademark mood swings. All that was left was this even, deadly temper.

He withdrew his hand, wiping the dampness from my hair onto a small white towel. "I'm sure you're worried," he said, "but the Council surgeon has checked you out. The bullet wounds in your side and arm are clean, though the one that clipped your chest does appear to have nicked a bone." He clicked his tongue. "We all know that one will take a while to heal."

He tossed the towel aside and stepped away from where I hung, his words fading in the background as I could suddenly see the room where I was being held.

"Sacrilege," I croaked out, but my voice was weaker than Morgan cared to take notice of.

"So you won't bleed out or anything, but I'm not quite ready to let you heal." The soles of his loafers were soundless on the gray tile floor of the archive. Somewhere behind me was the prophecy, encased in steel and glass. He indicated a tall man in his early twenties leaning arms-crossed against one of the low desks. "William here will be in charge of keeping you awake until the meeting."

He was baiting me, I realized. He needed to brag, to have some sort of audience for his scheme. I resisted the urge to struggle against the restraints at my wrists. They were bound over my head, and I was tied again at the waist and ankles.

He lowered his tone. "My sources tell me rumors are spreading about my new gift," he said. "A shame, really. I'd so wanted it to be a surprise."

My stomach turned.

"It's ironic, don't you think," he continued, "that the girl was under my nose the entire time." His pacing had stopped, and he leaned forward as a small smile crept onto his face. "We thought it was her mother, you see. Had her captive some time ago." He shrugged, leaned back to slide his hands casually into the slanted pockets of his slacks. "She possessed all the signs—her line, her eyes, her blood, and her power." His smile grew. "Oh, the power."

His right foot turned out as if he meant to resume pacing, but he couldn't take his eyes off my face, too eager for some recognition in my expression.

"She was no mere prophet," he said. "She had a gift. Something like no other." Morgan swallowed, glanced around the room. It was so unlike him. "Do you know what she could do?" he asked.

I couldn't respond, only stare at this cold, hard man who was once my brother.

"I didn't understand at first," he whispered. "I didn't, Aern. How could I?" For the first time since I'd seen him again, his eyes lit with something akin to pleasure. "But it was there. The moment I put her under sway, it was there." He shook his head. "She couldn't stop it. Gods but she tried."

His lip twitched. "It's incredible, Aern. You can't comprehend what it feels like." His hands came free of their pockets as he moved closer. "Somehow, some way, she was able to"—he searched for the right word—"connect these missing pieces from our past. She gave us back what we lost, brother. She gave us back the power."

The pain in my side was becoming more prevalent. It was as if I were being torn apart without him so much as tightening the ropes. My body knew what I needed to recover, and the urge to sleep was overwhelming. It took all of my focus just to process his speech. "What are you saying?" I asked wearily.

He sighed, disappointed with my lack of enthusiasm. "I'm saying it's all changed," he said. "I'm saying the prophet has given us something we could have never dreamt of." His words were not simply an explanation. Morgan had spent the whole of his life certain of the outcome, and this, whatever he was trying to tell me, had given him more than that expectation. Had given him something else, something better.

He leaned forward again. "Her gift is to unbind those powers that lie dormant in our magic, to connect our minds to those abilities we thought we had lost. It's not just the sway, Aern. We could have it all back. Everything."

Everything. The dominion our ancestors held over all. *The abilities.*

I stared at him, openly shaken, and he smiled again.

"There," he said, "you've finally got it. She released those gifts to me. It's taken some time to master, I'll admit, but she strengthened my sway. And all the while I thought she was the chosen. But she wasn't." He took a deep, regretful breath. "I would have kept her, Aern. I would have gotten more, but I didn't think. Because of the prophecy, I was certain our paths were set."

"You killed her," I accused. My voice was still quiet and raw, but it conveyed the disgust well enough.

He shook his head disapprovingly. "You're not listening. She couldn't stop herself from doing as I commanded under sway, she wasn't strong enough to fight it. But she worked out the single thing that would prevent us from using her." He shifted. "That was a hard time for me, Aern. I was highly disappointed in the turn it had taken. But I can see now. I'd thought she only meant to keep the prophecy from playing out. I thought I'd lost my rightful destiny. But I hadn't. Because she didn't kill herself merely to prevent me from becoming the One, she did it to save her daughter. She did it to protect the chosen, so that I would never find her.

"It might have worked," he continued, "if I had been a weaker man. I had thought the chosen was gone, the prophecy taken from me, but I didn't quit. I had this new power"—he preened—"and a plan to find more. We would search for the others of her bloodline, find any that might carry the trait. She might have changed the game, but we were still the strongest players. I only wanted an extra edge, but we found far more than we bargained for.

"And then to discover my brother had stolen her. My own blood, stealing my birthright to keep me from power." His tone dropped dangerously low. "I should have known you'd take her to those dogs. You turned on your own kind. You are no better than a Samuels." His jaw flexed, but he held himself under control. "I don't know what you thought you'd do, how you'd manage to keep her from me, but your maneuvers were only a waste of time and energy. All you've done is to help me, Aern. Your betrayal gave us the chance to weed out the sheep. Council is stronger now. All of it, finally, at last, *mine*."

He laughed, and the sound made me flinch. "And in a matter of days, the girl will be as well."

"She's gone," I rasped. "Nothing you can do will get her back."

Morgan leered at me before turning to walk from the room. "That's where you're wrong."

22

Trapped

I had plenty of time to think about what Morgan had said, because every attempt I made at falling asleep, William created some new form of torture to wake me. Presently, he'd slapped me, quite hard, and was standing in waiting to be certain it had taken.

"Okay," I said, forcing my eyes open. "I've got it."

His gaze narrowed on me.

I pursed my lips. "Listen, how about you let my arms down for a while—"

"Silence," he said tersely.

"Why? Morgan doesn't trust you to—"

My words cut off as he slapped me again, though I was

clearly awake. *Clearly*.

"Boy, he's sure got you—"

William backhanded me. This time my only response was to turn my head as I spat blood.

I would have to think of something else. I was tied near the center of the room, in plain view of not only William, but three other battle-trained men. I could only assume the cameras hidden among the library shelves were still operational, which meant several more guards watched my every move from the safety of Council's private security office. Between me and that office were untold sentries, key-coded locks, and alarms. They had placed me in the archive for a reason. It was the most secure room on the property.

I racked my brain for a way to disable the cameras, the four men, those blasted ties cutting off circulation to my hands, or any portion of said list, but my mind was too addled from lack of sleep. I wondered vaguely if Logan had realized I was missing, if he'd waited at the drop point, or if someone from the Division had found him. But I couldn't even be certain what day it was. Judging from the severity of my wounds, I might have only slept hours before Morgan had woken me. Or it might have been days.

I could remember the pain, a bullet tearing through my side, one cutting my chest and striking bone, another in my leg... and Emily. The flash of sneaker as she disappeared into the trees. I hoped she wasn't still sealed within the chamber. I hoped someone had gotten her out. Not Morgan, surely.

He would have said. He would have been proud.

And then his words were swimming through my mind again, and I couldn't fathom their full potential for harm. Brianna's mother had not merely been a prophet. She'd had the power to release our kind's abilities. And they had known. Brianna first, but Emily, the realization only coming as she'd spoken the words in my room, that their mother had been taken before Morgan had gotten this sway. This new power. Her sickness, her panic made sense now. But as she'd doubled over, I'd spotted her mark, and everything had changed.

And that was our one saving grace. No one knew but the three of us. No matter what happened, Morgan would not fulfill the prophecy. Even if he captured Brianna, if he tricked the Division into giving her up, if he used his sway against them, he would still have the wrong girl.

Emily was the chosen.

"You're going to die, traitor-boy," a voice hissed from beside me, "and your dragon blood can't do a thing to stop it."

I stared straight ahead, but I could see the man in question. He leaned back in his chair, thumb playing patiently over the hammer of his pistol where it lay on his leg. The barrel casually pointed in my direction, but there was no threat of him using it. It would be Morgan's doing, not one of these men.

A low grumbling laugh followed, but William cut him off. "Silence."

The laughter ceased, but the man's mouth remained tweaked in a nasty grin.

It didn't matter that the sway had turned them against me. I *had* betrayed them. I had left them to Morgan. Whatever happened now, I had destroyed the brotherhood. I had destroyed Council.

As I waited for Morgan to kill me, there was one comfort in which I found solace. He had taken everything from both sides of the battle, but he would never win.

Because he would never have the girl.

I must have stared at the door for hours. When it finally opened, it was Caleb who walked in. My strength was waning, though I knew the wounds were slowly being repaired. The need for sleep was crippling, but I managed to follow his movement across the room. He was giving direction to William. Something was ready, something about time…

"Caleb," I said, my voice hoarse from exhaustion and disuse.

He didn't respond when I called his name, simply finished his conversation with William. But when he turned to go, I caught a glimpse of his face. It was somehow vacant, lifeless, and I felt my heart sink at the memory of Brendan's words so many hours ago. Morgan had used his sway. Noah was dead. Caleb had submitted.

But there was something wrong with the way Caleb had appeared. The sway on humans was nearly unrecognizable. I wondered if Morgan had destroyed some part of his brain. I wondered if this sway was different, stronger. I wondered if it had only been hours since that report landed in Brendan's hands, or days—how long I had been hanging here. I wondered where Brianna and Emily were.

"Wake up!" William yelled as he slapped me across the face.

I jolted, opening eyes I'd been completely unaware had closed, and rasped, "I'm getting really tired of that."

"Not me," William answered in a low tone.

He jerked the ties at my arm, which wrenched my side and brought me back to life. Abruptly awake, I realized the other men had guns on me. And there were five of them now.

"Where are we going?" I asked.

"To witness your brother's destiny," he said. "Now, make one wrong move and you'll get another bullet hole in your chest." He pointedly jabbed a finger into the meat over my heart. "And this one won't heal so easily."

My arms fell from their bonds, for a moment numb and then suddenly stinging with sharp, needling pain. I rubbed my wrists, agony and relief warring at the act, while William unlatched the other restraints. When he released my waist, my knees gave, and I fell against a post of the structure they'd brought in to restrain me.

He threw a shirt at me. "Clean up. Morgan doesn't want you looking like a vagrant."

I glanced down, dried blood covering large portions of my torn jeans.

"Put the shirt on," William demanded. "No one will see your legs anyway."

My head jerked up to stare at him, but he was already walking toward the door. "Let's go, Archer. We've got a prophecy to carry out."

I slid one arm into the button-up shirt, but it took considerably more effort for the other arm. After fumbling with the middle three buttons, I gave up, leaving it loose at the neck and bottom hem.

"On your feet," one of the gunmen said from beside me, and I pushed unsteadily off the post to be led from the room, a guard clutching each arm, two following behind, and another between us and William in the lead.

Morgan had never underestimated me.

Several minutes later, I was thrust into restraints and seated on the raised, dark-mahogany platform running the front wall of Council's meeting hall. William had been right, my lower half was not visible from the hall, because in front of me was a short half wall meant to disguise electrical equipment and the like. The half walls were positioned at each end of the raised platform, and at the center, not twenty feet from where I waited, was the podium from which Morgan would be making his "presentation." The chairs had been removed, and Council men lined the outer, unadorned tan and burgundy walls of the hall. I was surprised to see that they seemed to be adhering to at least one of the old code: there were no weapons in conference.

I recognized many faces, though few of them risked a look in my direction. They were pointedly *not* looking at the man their leader had tied to a chair, a man who would likely soon meet some unfortunate end at the hands of his brother. What I did not see were the faces that had been my allies. Nowhere among the crowd were the men and women who had supported my rise to head of Council, who had hoped I would one day supplant Morgan.

"Ready, brother?"

Morgan's voice from beside me made me jump, and I questioned my faculties for not hearing his arrival. And then the slightest noise, the muffled whisper of a metal track, and I knew why. There was a hidden door behind us, an unmarked entrance that had not been there before. I mentally cursed, knowing he'd have modified the security throughout Council's walls, because his biggest threats were those who had left him, those who had been raised to know this place's secrets.

I opened my mouth to respond, but before I could get the words out, Morgan's face lit up in a grin. "Brendan, so glad you could make it."

I followed his gaze to the entrance opposite us, and stared in horror as the Division's eight walked through the door.

"Shut it, Archer," Brendan said, "I'm not in the mood for your antics."

Behind them, a dozen more came through the door, headed by Logan, and what I assumed were his best men.

It felt as if the episode were playing out in slow motion, as if I were caught in the depths of an ocean and couldn't find which way to swim out, could do nothing to stop what was coming. It was endless and frantic, a sinking, drowning sensation, and I was helpless to fight it. Had they not realized what they were doing? Had they not read the prophecy? They were outnumbered three to one in this room alone. They had no chance of winning.

I wanted to shout at them to run, but I couldn't seem to get air.

They would die here, all of them.

Brendan's gaze flicked briefly to me, and then back to the center of the platform where Morgan stood. "We want to make a trade."

Morgan laughed. "Oh, Samuels. You always were a dull boy." He clapped his hands and picked up his speech-giving tone again. "You are here today to witness the coming of the prophecy."

He took two steps forward. "I understand that you of this... Division," he said with disgust, "have been living on the notion that you have figured out a way to subvert the prophecy." Morgan's gaze narrowed the slightest fraction, taking in the assembly that watched his performance. "But I can assure you, you are wrong."

Brendan stared on, but several of the others shifted uncomfortably.

"Let me say, also," Morgan continued, "what a huge disappointment it has been that you turned against the core of our existence, the one truth of our kind." His eyes scanned the group of twenty. "That so many of you were traitors to our lines." Morgan shook his head, as if dismissing the idea. "No bother. Because most of you will not be leaving this room alive."

Brendan's jaw went tight. "You invoked the rules of the code, Morgan. You invited us here under the pretense of conference, and now you turn on the very ideals you accuse of us abandoning."

"Precisely," Morgan said. "You have abandoned them. Which is why they do not apply to you." He paused. "Some of you may stay," he added, gaze lingering on Kara, "but we will decide that later."

Kara swallowed hard, the thought of being wanted by Morgan suddenly worse than the threat of death.

"First," Morgan said, "to dispose of this notion that the heir can be your savior."

"Wait," Brendan said. "We can give you the girl. Set Aern free, and we will bring the chosen to you. The Drake girl is all that matters."

Morgan laughed. "Don't be a fool, Samuels. I don't need your help to find Brianna. And besides, once my brother is gone, there is no other way for things to play out. The prophecy will bring her to me."

"You'll have to kill us first," Logan said, stepping from behind Brendan to glare at my brother.

Morgan shrugged. "I could, but that wouldn't be as much

fun." He glanced pointedly around the room. "You see, I can pretty much do whatever I please."

I sickened at the reminder, suddenly sure that part of his display would include using the sway on one of us.

It was obvious the others were thinking the same. Logan's chest rose and fell in measured breaths. I was certain he was forming a plan, one that would unquestionably cost him his life. The drowning sensation became suddenly acute. We were running out of air. We didn't have long.

"Do it," I said to Morgan. "Quit trying to make a show of yourself and just get it over with."

"As you wish," Morgan said, slipping the thin silver blade from inside his jacket. He took two steps toward me.

"No!"

The shout came from across the room, and every eye in the place fell on the same spot as mine.

Relief and terror flooded me. The source of the command was the one person none of us expected. The one person who didn't appear to be a threat.

The one person who should have never been there.

Emily.

23

EDGES

She was wearing the same clothes I'd left her in, her white Henley smeared with dirt and blood, and she'd slammed into the conference hall much in the way she'd slammed into that warehouse on our first meeting. Morgan froze, visibly stunned, and there I sat, once again caught, bound, and powerless to sway her.

My gaze shot to Logan in a silent attempt for assistance, to beg him to remove her, but he just lifted his shoulders in a helpless shrug. Brendan looked furious, the rest of the room simply confused.

Recognition dawned on Morgan's face, and he smiled, abruptly returning to his show. "Ah, and here's the infamous sister. Such a pleasure you could join us."

The implication in his tone tore through me and I was suddenly sitting upright, struggling vainly against my bonds. He would use her now. He would have Brianna.

Damn it, why had she come? It had been the one thing that kept me sound. The chosen was protected. Emily was safe.

Morgan turned and stepped closer to the edge of the platform, and the first drops of blood seeped through my fisted palms as they writhed beneath the restraints.

"No," I hissed at Morgan's back. "Leave them be."

He didn't turn but I could see the side of his jaw flex as his grin increased.

"Take the trade," Emily said levelly from across the room. "If he dies here today, you will never get Brianna."

Gods, what was she doing? She meant to threaten him?

"Well, well," Morgan hummed. "What a puerile group of admirers you have here, brother." He glanced over his shoulder at me, both of us knowing they were at his mercy. Neither of us doubting every single one would soon die. "Kind of pathetic, isn't it?"

"Let them go, Morgan," I said. "Let them go and I will follow you. I will submit."

He smirked at the desperation in my voice, my clenched teeth. His gaze fell briefly to the blood trickling down my palms to pool on the floor, but he wasn't concerned that I might escape.

"So," Morgan said for the crowd, "you come here to make demands of me, little commonblood."

Emily stepped forward, separating herself from the crowd at the entrance, centering her position between the Council men lining the walls. "I am giving you your last chance," Emily said. She stared, unshaken, at the man who had killed her mother. The man who had held her mother captive, forced her into the only choice that could save her daughters' lives.

Morgan shook his head, disbelief clear in his tone. "You people stand here as if you have some kind of say in the matter." He gestured toward the door, the men lining the walls. "Do you think I've not covered these rooms with the highest security? Do you think I've not filled those halls with guns, with trained men who plan to stop each of you from leaving the property?" His voice dropped to a deadly tone. "Do you think that I cannot move you all at my will?"

Emily took a deep breath, and then gripped the handle of a blade that was strapped beneath the front hem of her shirt. *Four knives*, I thought, *for gods' sake, she has four knives.*

Her left hand dropped in a strange motion, and I suddenly stilled. My eyes found Logan, who had eased slightly away from the other Division men. My stomach dropped, and instinctively, my mouth opened to stop them. But I couldn't. There was nothing I could do. Any signal I gave would only alert Morgan. Her right hand came up, her grip loose and ready.

Morgan laughed. "Oh, look, Aern. Your prom queen brought a knife." His words were light, plainly unconcerned she could strike him from that distance, and several of the younger men along the walls chuckled. But I could see the concentration in his features, the way his thumb pressed against the inside of the platinum ring at the base of his third finger. It wasn't working. He was doing everything in his power to sway this girl, and it wasn't working.

My chest swelled. He couldn't take her. He could never steal her mind. I prayed he wouldn't kill her, that he would wait, try and use her to bait Brianna, that there was some chance...

And then the corner of Emily's mouth rose in a smirk, as if she, too, were laughing at his prom queen jab. When her knife landed solidly into the left side of his chest, it was as if all the air was sucked from the room.

"I was homeschooled," she said evenly, a new knife suddenly in her hand, and I knew the words were to remind him of her mother.

Morgan let out a shocked huff of air, hand coming up to grip the hilt protruding from his chest, and the room broke into chaos.

"Here," Logan shouted to the men behind him, pointing the location of a concealed keypad. Several soldiers moved on the group, whose position now seemed less like cattle being led to slaughter and more like a raging stampede. Brendan reached behind his back to retrieve a hidden revolver, apparently not so trusting as he had seemed, but shots were fired from the opposite side of the room and there was abruptly a frenzy of suits and soldiers searching for cover, aiming for kills, and locked in unarmed brawls.

Two men leapt onto the stage to grab Morgan, who had removed the blade and was screaming furious threats at anyone within earshot. I had broken loose of one restraint, but dislocated a thumb in the process and couldn't free my other hand.

I yelled, *"No!"* toward Emily as she rushed the stage, but it couldn't be heard over the din of battle.

Her eyes met Morgan's as he was dragged behind the hidden door, each of them delivering an unspoken promise before the panel slid closed and broke their connection.

"Look out!" I screamed, and she rolled to the floor just as one of Morgan's men took a shot at her from the lower level. He spun as a bullet tore through his chest, and she crawled over to cut my straps free.

"What are you doing?" I hissed as she cut the last tie and I could finally grab and shake her.

She stared helplessly for a moment, as if she had no good answer, and then I fell to the ground as my legs collapsed.

A cry escaped Emily and she crumpled over me. Panting, I looked down where her hand pressed tight against my hip, and realized I'd been shot. Again.

"Help!" Emily yelled. "Logan! Brendan!" and then, as though she could think of no other name, "Eric!"

I took a deep breath, and then pressed my own hand over hers and leaned forward.

"Aern," Logan said, suddenly crouched in front of us.

I nodded and Emily slid her hand from under mine, and then she and Logan each took a shoulder.

"The east wall," Logan said, and we moved clumsily across the platform toward the steps. Two of Logan's men met us there, covering fire and helping to block our escape from view. As we came to the east entrance, I glanced at Logan, who seemed to know more than anyone else about the new ins and outs of Council.

"I'd already done the recon," he said, gesturing at Emily as he released my shoulder. She was on my good side, and slipped easily beneath my arm to prop me up while he pressed a code into the keypad. Emily glanced at the other entrance, the one currently blocked by thirty of Council's men, at the shouting and fighting and gunfire, and then, with a sick expression, impatiently back at Logan.

The door slid open and we were shuffling down the hall in an attempt at running, the two other men splitting up to scout ahead and cover our backs. Three downed guards littered the floor of the corridor.

"We broke in earlier," Logan explained. "Took out the ones Morgan had planned to surprise us with, disabled some of their security systems. I would have done more, but we didn't have long before we had to meet up and enter with Brendan. Couldn't leave them alone." We turned a corner. Two more men lay prostrate along the walls. "Most of them were tranquilizer darts," he said, glancing sidelong at me as we moved. "The men weren't quite ready to kill their brothers."

"Down!" the scout yelled from the corner to the hallway in front of us. We crouched, Logan releasing my arm to ready his pistol, and gunfire erupted ahead of us.

Emily flinched as a bullet ripped through the arm of our frontman's jacket. Several more rounds were fired, and then he turned to signal our backup before waving us forward.

"How much farther?" Emily asked, and I realized I was weighing a little too heavily on her slender frame.

Logan pressed a finger against his ear, and said, "Not much, they've got clearance at the northeast corner."

Gunfire and shouting echoed behind us, and Logan picked up the pace to nearly drag me with them. Three Division men appeared in the corridor in front of us, guns at the ready, and ushered us the last ten feet to a door. Sunlight burst into the foyer, and I squinted, snow-blind as they rushed me across the lawn. More gunfire, the chopping sound of helicopter blades, the barking of orders, torturous groans from the wounded, and then I was face down on leather and Emily was curled into the floorboard beneath me.

I reached for her, my hand clutching hers tightly, and promptly passed out from loss of blood.

24

Mending

I smelled Emily's shampoo, and my mouth turned up at the corners. I was lying face down on clean cotton sheets, one arm under pillows, the other draped over the side of a bed. When I opened my eyes, she was inches away, watching me.

"Hi," I said in a gravelly voice.

She bit her lip and swallowed hard. "Hi."

The bedding beneath me was a deep shade of burgundy, and I knew we were no longer in the Fordham house. I glanced briefly around the room. Antique cherry dresser, highly ornate vintage armoire—this would be Southmont.

"How are you?" I asked Emily, and a shaky, breathless laugh

escaped her. She'd been watching me for how long? Worried because I'd been shot. I rolled to my side to face her, cupped a hand on her cheek. "I'm fine."

She was suddenly crying, and I pulled her to me for a hug. "What is it?" I whispered. "Is it Brianna?"

She tilted her head to look at me, wiping absently at her cheek. "No, I... I'm sorry. Everything is fine." She took a deep breath. "Brianna is downstairs. She's had a lot of work to do, but she's fine. Everyone, everyone is fine."

I sat up, keeping her near as I moved to question her.

She waved a hand. "Logan said you would ask. He said they were trained men, but never hit a lethal mark. Something about brotherhood"—she took another deep breath, this one seemed to steady her—"and that Morgan hadn't prepared them ahead of time. He said to tell you that was what saved us." A bit of guilt crossed her face and she looked away.

"What else, Emily?"

She sighed heavily. "And me," she said. "He said to tell you me."

Relief flooded me, but I managed to narrow my eyes on her. "So you have Logan taking your side now?"

Her gaze swept up to mine, still damp with tears, and I could see her repentance. "It was so stupid," she said. "I could have messed up everything."

"It was stupid," I said, bringing her chin back up. "But thank you."

My wrists were clean and smooth. I stretched, testing out my side. "I feel great, actually. How long was I out?"

She glanced at the clock. "About six hours," she said.

"No, I mean altogether."

She looked at the clock once more, nodding. "Yeah, that's about right. The doctors stitched you up a bit." She glanced down, twisting the hem of her clean white shirt. "They made me go take a shower." She looked sick at the memory of leaving me, shot in five or six places, and then swallowed hard. "And then Brianna saw you."

It seemed to be an explanation, though at first I couldn't understand why. This amount of damage, surgeon or no, should have taken much, much longer to heal. And then, slowly, her words fell together. Brianna was downstairs, she had a lot of work to do, but everyone was fine.

I stared at her.

She nodded.

I closed my eyes for one long moment, remembering the words they'd shared in the tunnel before our escape. Brianna had said she bore her mother's gifts. Plural. An image of the wounds Emily had left on my arms came then, and the way they'd healed in minutes instead of days. Without the benefit of sleep.

"Brianna is a healer," I breathed. I should have felt it in her touch, should have known.

"No," Emily said, confused.

"But..." I glanced down, feeling nothing but well. "How..."

She grimaced. "Brianna didn't heal you, Aern." She placed a hand over my palm. "She *fixed* you."

I sat still for so long, Emily's head tilted, as if she wasn't certain I was behind my vacant stare.

When I blinked, she spoke again. "She made those connections, Aern. The ones our mother taught her to." I opened my mouth with a horrified protest, but she stopped me. "Not all of them, not the ones with the influence," she explained. "Just to help you all heal faster."

"Oh, Emily," I breathed. "She should never have done that. Brendan, the others, if they know she has this—"

She held up a hand, stopping me again. "It isn't like that, Aern. They already suspected she had a gift, but they don't know. They don't truly understand." She glanced around the room, and I could tell she was speaking with caution. "They simply think she can help them recover faster. That's all."

Her eyes spoke more than her words could. None of them knew she was a prophet. None of them knew she could affect their sway. They didn't know how their mother had died, that Brianna could give them Morgan's power. That Emily was the chosen.

She let me process the information for a very long time, sitting silently before me, hand still resting patiently within mine. After everything that had happened, everything that could still come about, she was here.

The scope of it all fell into place. I was one of them, one of the monsters she'd been warned her whole life to stay away from, to protect Brianna from, and she had risked everything to save me. I yearned to draw her closer, to touch her face once more, gods, to press my lips to hers. But it was a betrayal.

I gripped her shoulders, placing her several inches back from where I sat. The action troubled her, but I held firm. "Emily," I said, "there is something I have to tell you. I should have told you long ago." My chest tightened. This was going to crush her. "It was about Brianna." I rubbed a hand over my forearm. "But now it concerns you."

She waited, distress playing across her features.

"The reason Morgan wanted Brianna—" Gods, how did I explain this? "The way that he needs her…"

Emily nodded. "The prophecy. They would create a union."

"A bond," I said. "An actual, tangible link."

She moved closer. "I know, Aern. I understand. But Morgan will never have me."

I stiffened, completely thrown by her words. By the idea of Morgan… "No," I said, pushing her back. "That's not what I'm trying to say."

She stayed this time, waiting for me to finish.

"Not Morgan," I explained. "The Division. The reason they want me, the reason they've been after me for so long"—I found my gaze wandering, focusing on anything but the expression on her face—"is that they've read the prophecy differently." My throat went dry. "They think that the union, this bond, can be created by any heir to the dragon's name. By either Morgan…" My eyes met hers. "Or me."

She sat silent for an eternity of seconds, then said, "I know."

I stared at her. And then, "What?"

"I know," she said. "My mother told me, some time ago." She shrugged. "I just didn't think it would be me, is all." Her voice dropped lower. "But it is me. And I'm glad, Aern. I'm glad that it is me, and that it's you."

A rush of emotion, too fast, too broad to sort into anything, surged through me, and I was moving for her. She had known. All along, she had known.

I pulled her into my embrace, and she drew tighter against me. She had been waiting for this, since I had found her mark, she had accepted it. Her arms around my shoulders, I pressed my lips hard against hers, regaining all of those moments I'd denied myself the touch, and she melted into me, her breath a soft moan of relief. The kiss was deep, fire and passion and unpinned desire. My hands slid lower down her back, squeezing her to me, and she slid her legs over mine. She smelled of sweet pea and strawberries, and something all her own.

Her head tilted back as she tried to catch her breath and I trailed kisses down the line of her neck, stopping just above her chest, at the tiny divot centering her collarbone, to collect myself. She was mine, she was in my arms, and she was mine.

My hand slipped beneath the hem of her shirt, finding the heat of her lower back as my mouth skimmed over her throat on its return to hers. The kiss became gentle, teasing, and soft. My hand slid over the length of her thigh, and then up, touching the skin between her open collar, the pulse hammering at the base of her neck, and into the caramel waves of her hair. Her eyes came open, hazy and gratified, and the soft, deep green of the sea. Our lips drew apart and we simply watched one another, both of us knowing we could stare into these eyes forever, and then it happened. And it was a coming home.

It was peace, settling deep within my chest, a feeling of rightness. It made me whole, and it threatened to tear me apart. A longing so intense it was painful tore at me, and I knew I would never get enough of her. I could never leave her. It would always be Emily.

Emily.

I realized I'd spoken then, murmured her name, and she gasped.

"Did you feel that?" she whispered.

We sat pressed together, face to face, but it was as if our souls were suddenly seamed, bound so tightly as to be one.

"It's the bond," I said.

She stared at me in stunned astonishment. "It's like, like my insides are tied."

I automatically gave her space. "Is that what it feels like to you?"

I could hear the worry in my tone, and I realized I'd been afraid of what it would be for her. None of the elders had known how the bond would affect the chosen, what it would do to one without our power.

Panic slammed into me. *What if it has enslaved her? Like the sway.*

She blinked, searching my face. "No, it's like... Like lacing up a good pair of running shoes—"

The fear waned at her denial, but when her words sank in, the short-lived determination to hold my expression faltered.

"... that feeling, when you have them good and snug," she said, her gesturing hand falling to rest over my heart. "That security."

My chest eased. I felt a tug at the corner of my mouth. I cleared my throat. "Did you just compare our bond to running shoes?"

She stared at me a moment, searching for a better comparison for something so indescribable. Her brow curved speculatively. "A five-point racing harness?"

I laughed, and then pulled her closer. The words felt right in the old tongue, and I knew she would understand them. Loosely translated, the sentiment was something like, "love's embrace," as I spoke them low, to the only woman who would ever hear them again.

Her skin flushed and she repeated them back before leaning forward, suddenly desperate for another kiss.

25

STRATEGY

We lay together, my thumb pressed into the crook of her elbow, fingers wrapped around her skin, while my lips traced feather light kisses down the line of her jaw.

"Aern," she whispered, trying to bring my attention to the insistent knock at the door.

I released her arm and slid my hand lower, to the bend of her knee, drawing it firmly over my hip. "It doesn't matter," I said, pressing slow kisses to the delicate skin below her ear. "Nothing else matters."

She sighed, but it was the wrong kind of sigh. She pressed a hand against my chest to look at me, a grimace forming on her perfect lips. "I'm afraid it does matter," she said.

I waited, fighting the urge to continue my explorations.

"It's Morgan," she said.

I cleared my throat. That was a mood-killer. "What do you mean?"

"The knife was too low," she groused. "He's been forming an attack since earlier this afternoon."

I leaned up on an elbow.

"He's a little upset, Aern. And he's coming to"—she winced—"finish us off."

"Finish us off?" I said.

She smirked. "His words, not mine. Listen, I got us some time together, but Logan can only cover us for so long."

I sat up. "What on Earth are you talking about?"

She looked pointedly toward the door. "What were we supposed to do? No one knows about Brianna, so they didn't want us together."

"Dammit, Aern," Logan hissed from outside the door. "Open up."

I fell back to the mattress, hand slapping loosely over my face.

"Don't worry," Emily said. "I'll get it."

A minute later, Logan's voice hovered above me. "I know you're awake."

I dropped the hand to glare at him.

"Brendan is sending someone to retrieve you," he said. "We've only got hours to prepare."

I hadn't even gotten dressed yet. I looked down, pursing my lips at hospital-issue Ralph Lauren pajamas. I glanced at Emily where she stood behind Logan, still fully dressed and only mildly disheveled. "Thirty more minutes," I said.

She flushed, ran a hand over her hair.

"No deal," Logan said. "The only reason I got talked into this, was because you needed to recover. But now I'm out. Brendan isn't catching me leaving you alone in here with…" He started to gesture toward Emily, and then cleared his throat. "Besides, you need to catch up."

"Fine," I said. "Get started."

Logan gave me a quick debriefing while I rummaged through the dresser, and then I took a three-minute shower while they waited. As I rinsed off, I marveled at the raised pink skin lining my hip and side, the only remainder of what was surely a handful of gruesome injuries. Aside from some muscle tightness over what was likely still reforming bone, I was almost completely recovered. I slipped on a white tee, loose-fit jeans, and brown leather belt and shoes. Morgan would be here soon, in his custom-made suit and tie, and I didn't want to disappoint him.

When I returned to the main room, Seth was waiting for us. "A few of Morgan's men have been spotted along the borders of our outlying properties," he explained. "Brendan thinks it's a ploy, to get us to move our men from covering home base. But regardless, we'll still need to shield them." He glanced at Emily. "We have people there who need protection."

"I'll be heading to the Adair house," Logan said. "I've got enough men to cover the files and what staff remain on site. Team two will return to Fordham, and the Westlake properties will be evacuated until we have a better idea of what their plans are." He gave me a long look. "Be safe, brother."

I returned the sentiment with a terse nod, and then said, "We'll talk later," putting more meaning in words that would sound to Seth like a generic reply. Logan was no fool, but he didn't understand what was happening with Emily. And the thought brought pause, because I'd barely had time to process it myself.

My gaze found hers, and I could tell by the way her cheeks colored she was thinking along similar lines. And then both of us realized we were being watched, and we broke the connection to say goodbye to Logan and be escorted to the meeting by Seth.

The Southmont house was large, even by Division standards, and was much like a colonial museum. The colors were rich, carpeting plush, and furnishings ornate dark woods. Oil portraits lined the corridors and elaborate battle scenes or landscapes featured the long walls of open, spacious rooms. The house had a history, and we were about to add to it.

Seth led the way, walking the halls in front of us, and I let my arm brush Emily's, unable to resist the urge for at least some contact. When we at last neared the entrance to the conference room, she froze, a hint of panic in her tone. "Wait."

Seth stopped, glancing over his shoulder in a half turn.

I waved him on. "Go ahead, we'll be there in a minute."

As soon as the door closed, she was in my arms, both of us in great need of one last touch. I squeezed her tight to me as we moved, until she was pressed against the wall and I could free my grip. She reached around my shoulders to bring herself higher, desperate to deepen the kiss, and my hands slid low to curve around her thigh and raise her off the ground. Her fingers were suddenly grasping at the hem of my shirt as she struggled to pull it free, to press her skin to mine. When she finally succeeded, her touch, her bare palms exploring the skin of my chest, my back, crossing my abdomen, sent fire through me. My hips pressed into hers and she groaned.

It took everything I had to pull away from her.

I leaned back, both of us breathless, and stared into her heavy-lidded eyes.

A wry smile crossed her lips as she realized we were still in the hall. She cleared her throat, and slowly withdrew her legs from around my waist to slide down the wall. My head leaned forward to press against hers, and then I found her mouth again, for two soft kisses. Her hands slipped from beneath my shirt, one gliding slowly up my chest to rest over my heart while the other circled my back in a tender embrace. And we simply stayed there. It was too long, and it would never be enough.

As the voices rose from within the conference room, Emily sighed, and I leaned further back to take her hand. I brought it up for a brief kiss, and then held it until the last moment, when the door finally opened in front of us.

The conference room was large, poorly lit, and packed full of Division men. Brendan stood front and center, fielding questions and sorting out arguments. Brianna was off to the side, sitting watch at what appeared to be the only isolated area of the room. With Wesley.

Though he didn't acknowledge it, Wesley excused himself from Brianna's side as we entered the room. We made our way over, and Emily took his seat on Brianna's left as I slid onto the table, one foot resting on the bench to her right.

We listened as Brendan laid out a plan, giving specific, detailed directions to each of his men, covering every entrance and exit to the property, to the house. He didn't miss one single aspect, didn't skip over one single point. They were coming, and he would go over it until the last minute. It would be learned by rote.

It wasn't long before Emily became restless, standing, shifting, and then pacing the back and side walls of the conference room.

I tried not to watch her, leaning forward as I sat on the table, elbow resting just above my knee, thumb twisting the ring on my middle finger.

Brianna didn't look at me as she spoke. "It's not going to work."

"No," I said, though the certainty I felt was not the work of prophecy. It was merely familiarity with Morgan.

"She will save us," Brianna said. "But not this time."

My thumb stilled against the ring. "Brianna—"

She turned to me then, so close beside me, and the wanness in her face stopped me short. "It keeps shifting," she said with a sad smile. "It's never done that before."

I glanced automatically at Emily.

"Yes," Brianna said. "I suppose I should have thought of that, given that none of the prophecies went past the union."

She took a deep breath and my eyes came back to hers, questioning.

"I'm just tired," she said.

"Come on," I said, stepping down from my seat. "There's no reason for us to be here."

When I grasped her hand, several of the observers across the room took notice. But it didn't bother me now, because none of that mattered. The union was complete.

And nothing about it felt wrong.

26

Resistance

"It's time."

The voice from the doorway came much too soon. The three of us had been waiting in one of the small sitting rooms, knowing what was coming. Knowing we had gotten lucky before. It wouldn't happen again. This time, people would die.

And none of us were ready for that.

Brianna squeezed her sister's hand, and then gave me a meaningful look before joining Seth at the door. "I'd like to see Brendan privately for a moment. Aern and Emily can meet us there."

Seth's gaze swept over us, but he didn't argue with Brianna.

When they were gone, I stood and crossed to Emily where she sat perched on the edge of a low-backed chaise, pretending to study a painting. I held out a hand and she took it, silently standing to move into my embrace.

She slipped her arms around my back, and we stayed there, unspeaking, as I pressed a kiss to the top of her head.

I wouldn't let it be the last time.

"I'm not scared," Emily whispered against my chest.

I leaned back, lifting her chin to face me.

"But I can't shake this feeling," she said. "The prophecy, we can't trust it, can we?" She shifted, her hand coming to rest on my side. "Have we brought absolute conflict? Blood against blood? Or is there more? They were so wrong, about everything, Aern. It was all there, and they'd only misunderstood."

"It doesn't matter," I said. "We've created the bond. We will find a way to get through this."

"Will we?" she asked in a soft voice. "Because I don't know anymore. What if we've mistaken it this time? The heir to the dragon's name will rule with the union. They were wrong about which heir before—"

"No," I said, cutting her off too abruptly, and she narrowed her gaze. If I had been sure, it wouldn't have been so harsh.

"You heard Brianna," she said. "Morgan can't die. Not yet." She glanced toward the doorway. "If he still has a part to play, Aern..."

"No," I repeated. He would not have her. No matter what else happened, Morgan would not win.

Her breath came out heavily and she stared at me. Finally, she nodded, adopting my determination as she straightened to go.

"Wait," I said, grabbing her arm to pull her to me. I studied her for a long minute, re-memorizing her features. And then I touched my lips against hers softly, lingering there to whisper her name. When I pulled away, her eyes remained closed, saving the moment, and then steeling herself for what was to come.

Brendan's office had been transformed. Forty of Division's men stood scattered around a control room of sorts, sleek, flatscreen monitors and communication equipment covering every flat surface near the back wall. A spiderweb of wires crisscrossed the desks and tables, historic furniture now overwrought with electronic technology. Cables vined up through the stand of an old-fashioned writing desk, supplying the computer systems Eric's younger brother ran. Plush, burgundy carpet held the restless feet of cultivated soldiers, waiting for battle.

The chairs sat empty.

No one spoke; the time for words was over. There was nothing but the wait. And then it was gone.

"He's here," Brendan said from his place behind the display.

The room fell still.

"North wall. He's using the main entrance." He glanced at the other screens. "They haven't split up. He's bringing them all together."

Beside me, I felt Brianna's lack of surprise. I couldn't look at her, though, because Emily was there, standing on her other side.

"Cue the gate current," he said. "I don't know what he's got up his sleeve."

The boy keyed in the command, sending high voltage through the secondary barriers near the gate, and we all watched as a dozen black town cars and sleek new SUVs pulled to a stop in front of the wall. The driver of the second car stepped out, opening the door behind him for Morgan.

He stood, elegant in black suit and tie, and straightened his jacket with a practiced shrug. His hands went to his wrist, adjusting his cuffs with an easy smile. Right into the camera.

"Brendan," I said, but my voice was too low, too lost in the realization.

"What's happening?" Kara yelled. "Brendan, damn it, why are they letting him in?"

Brendan's head pivoted as he switched from one screen to another, examining the angles, willing it not to be true.

The gates swung open, and Morgan waved the cars forward as he slid back into his own vehicle. Light flashed off tinted glass as the door shut behind him, and his driver returned to his station.

"Stop them," Eric said as the first car drove through.

Keys clicked furiously as another command was entered, but they had expected to find them on foot, not driving through the main gate.

We watched in horrified silence as the progression of vehicles made its way up the drive, bypassing every security precaution laid before them.

Brendan was speechless at his own mistake. But it was all of us who'd overthought it. There was no way to stop what was happening, it was too late to undo this now.

A wave of black doors opened down the drive as Morgan's men stepped from their cars. They were relaxed and confident, armed with silencers and long-range weapons. Morgan walked forward, heading casually toward the steps of the mansion.

"Shoot him," Brendan said, his hand pressed against the device in his ear.

The command went unanswered as Morgan's gaze swept the men outside the front entrance. Seven shots were fired, but the cameras caught Division men falling, not Morgan.

"The sway," Eric whispered. "Gods, he's turning our men with a single glance."

"Set a sniper," Brendan demanded. "Get someone out of his sight and waiting at the main door, *now!*"

Two of the cameras showed their response, a half dozen men scrambling to change position, set up to fire on him. But they couldn't kill him, Brianna had said. I glanced sideways at her, but she wasn't watching. Whatever Brendan did now, he did under his own conscience, because Brianna was elsewhere, her pupils flickering against a sea-green iris. My gaze fell to Emily, hand resting on the hilt of her blade through the fabric of her shirt as she watched Brendan go against her sister's advice.

We'd not revealed Brianna's gift to anyone else. Only Brendan knew she was a prophet. To speak it now would put her in more danger.

I opened my mouth to call Brendan's attention, but stopped short as my gaze caught on a screen.

"No," he hissed as a Division soldier rushed a sniper set to fire on Morgan. Kara's hands flew up to cover her mouth as a bullet from his own team ripped through his chest. A second monitor flashed as another Division man shot a gunman in the stomach and then turned to fire on the camera. Brendan frantically called orders over his headset, but it was too late. The soldiers from the gate and front entrance were moving through the house, taking down strategically placed men who were out of Morgan's range.

He wasn't even using his own army. He had turned ours against us.

I didn't look at Emily as I ran. I wasn't sure I could go through with this if I had. But Morgan had to be stopped, and there was only one chance, one person who might have the ability to stand up to his power without risking her and her sister.

"Stop!" Brianna shouted from behind me, but I couldn't look at her. I had to do this. I waited in the doorway, hands pressed against the frame.

"He cannot die," Brianna said to my back. "You can stop him, Aern. But he cannot die."

27

CHALLENGE

In the end, it was all of us who ran to meet him. We could not stand to watch another soldier die, could not wait idly by as they slaughtered the lot of us. And so we stood, a room full of descendants of the seven lines, and faced Morgan.

"No more," Brendan said, his words echoing off the walls of what was once a ballroom. "You've killed enough."

Morgan smiled. "Oh, but I'm just getting started." He raised a hand casually to the men on our right, though they'd followed Brendan's command to lower their weapons.

"You've won, Morgan," I said. "You've made your point."

He turned to look at me, but the hand didn't immediately

drop. The expression on his face made it perfectly clear he was aware of his victory. "I'm not done yet, brother."

His eyes fell to the men standing beyond his hand, and their rifles rose. Emily flinched beside me when the first shots fired, and I couldn't help but to reach for her, press her slightly behind me. It was a mistake, and Morgan noticed. He waved a hand and the firing ceased. Seven more Division men lay bleeding on the polished wood floor. But they were not kill shots. Not yet.

Kara's hand pressed to her stomach, several of the others looked as if they too might be sick. Morgan was going to drag this out, he was reveling in the power.

"My, my," he crooned, "it seems you finally care about someone, brother." His eyes trailed slowly over Emily before returning to mine. "Aside from yourself." His grin turned feral. "It will definitely make things more interesting."

My stomach plunged. He was going to hurt Emily. Because I'd touched her, tried to protect her, he would torture her. And he would be certain I stayed alive long enough to watch.

"I care about everyone here, Morgan." It took every ounce of energy not to let my tone betray the anger and tension blistering through me. "As should you."

He scoffed. "You are a fool."

"Just like our father?" I said.

His eyes flashed with rage, but before he could act, he remembered himself, realized I was trying to distract him.

"Come, girl," he said to Emily where she stood partially behind me. I couldn't see her face, but by the expressions reflected on Morgan's men, I knew she was anything but frightened.

Morgan snapped his fingers and the man to his left fired on a young boy behind us. He screamed out, the bullet having ripped through his thigh and knocked him off his feet. He wasn't strong. It wouldn't heal quickly enough.

Morgan's eyes fell back, not to Emily's, but mine.

Daring me.

He gave us two more seconds, and then snapped again. The report sounded, and even I almost started as it ripped through the shoulder of a man not three feet from us. Four seconds this time, and then the pistol swung to face Seth.

That broke her. An instant before Morgan's finger fell against his palm, Emily stepped from behind me.

"No!" Brianna yelled.

My heart dropped. Morgan smiled, his gaze slowly moving to where Brianna stood, separate from the others. She'd been the only one safe. The only one he wouldn't risk shooting.

He needed her.

"She's immune to your sway," Brianna said. "We both are."

Emily's hand shifted to her back, but I stilled it. This was no time to stab Morgan, not when he'd turned the whole of his army against us. At least she still had a chance. She, and Brianna, could live.

Brianna's shoulders straightened, and her eyes roamed Morgan's men. "You can't make us bend to your will," she said. "You've proven that."

Morgan slipped a hand casually into the pocket of his slacks, as if her speech was no more than entertainment.

"If you kill another," she said, "I will not go with you. Ever." She stepped forward. "What you had in my mother will be lost to you. Again."

At her final threat, he took pause.

Brianna gave him a moment to fully appreciate her words. And then, "I will submit to you, to save the others." She took a deep, steadying breath, willing this last-ditch effort to work, making this one sacrifice that would take everything from her. "It's the only way, Morgan. Reverse the sway, and I will go with you freely."

The muscles on Emily's arm tensed completely, but I held her in my grip. If Morgan accepted this, it would give them all a chance. He wouldn't hurt Brianna. Not until he knew.

I squeezed, hoping to somehow convey the idea that this could buy us time. We could rescue her. Before he tried the union, she could escape.

Morgan's head tilted to the side, considering her offer.

Brianna took another step forward. "I can give it all to you," she said. "Everything my mother did."

After a moment, he laughed, a kind of joyous, disbelieving chuckle, and then raised his hands. "Deal." He smiled. "But my brother comes with us."

Emily's hand fell from her blade, and her head jerked to stare at me. She knew, without a doubt, that I would go. I had to, to save her. To save Brianna.

It was the only way.

And I would not show Morgan my weakness for her again.

"Release them," Brianna said as I walked forward.

Morgan shook his head absently at her demand, but glanced briefly at the men surrounding them. When his gaze returned to Brianna, he held out a hand.

She didn't move. "All of them."

A guilty smile lifted the corner of his mouth, and he tipped his head in a nod before turning back to his men. I wondered how Brianna knew, if this was part of her gift, or if she was bluffing.

Morgan concentrated harder this time, even laying hands on several of the men.

When he finally turned back to her, Brianna met us at the center of the room, where I stayed a few paces back from my brother.

He indicated the men should go, but then stopped, holding up the first finger of his left hand. "One more thing."

The flash of metal caught my eye a split second before the realization of what he was about to do kicked in. To anyone else, it might have seemed he was merely returning Emily's blade, but to me, it was a certainty. Morgan had never dealt with knives enough to know how to properly wield one, and the looseness in his grip told me in the last few hours, he'd learned. Not well enough to be a marksman, but enough to kill Emily, even at this distance, and he'd done so specifically for this. To return the injury she'd given him. I was acting without thought, flying through the air to tackle him and break the wrist that held her blade.

Brianna gasped as we landed at her feet, Council and Division men shuffling in the confusion of an instant's events. They stared on at Morgan's bloody nose, his torn shirt, the knife that now lay beside us as my hands wrapped tightly around his throat. I didn't know what was happening behind me. I didn't see Emily's response. All I knew was that this monster that had once been my brother was not going to heal out of this. He would not take another breath.

But something *had* happened. Something in Emily's gaze or something in the strength of my reaction, or some unknown trigger caused Morgan to come out of the immediacy of the fight, to understand my response. It was as if I could see it click. Deep within his eyes, he *knew*.

His face was purpling, but his eyes stared past me, and when they returned, it was no question he saw the bond. He knew what the Division had planned. He knew there was another way. And he could see it wasn't Brianna, but Emily. The girl immune to his sway. The girl he'd tried to kill.

The struggle went out of his limbs, but not because he was giving up. He went slack, because he was using all of his focus on something else. His hands rested on my forearms as the rage swept through him. If he couldn't win, no one would.

When the idea came into my head, I could do nothing to stop it. Because it was my thought now. My objective. I was powerless as my grip on Morgan let go to find and grasp the knife beside us. Time stilled, but it did nothing to save me. I couldn't scream. I couldn't warn her. My movements were swift, too practiced, too fast, and in a fraction of a second, and I was standing in front of Brianna. No one realized she was in danger. No one knew to stop me. My left arm braced her shoulder and my right swung true. I could do nothing else.

I could do nothing else.

Brianna stared into my eyes as her blood ran down my arms, rushing warm and wet through my hands, over the hilt of the blade I had stabbed beneath her chest.

"It was the only way," she breathed.

28

Recompense

Somewhere behind me there was a scream. Brianna's legs gave, and I caught her, speechless as I wrapped my arms around her. Brendan was suddenly there, taking her free of my grasp, and Emily, gods, Emily.

Emily was screaming.

"Get her to a hospital! For Christ's sake, help her!" She frantically searched the room for someone to respond, and then Brianna's hand slipped over hers and their gazes locked. "She can't heal," Emily whimpered. "She's not like you. She needs a doctor."

Brendan was shouting orders, and Division men were rushing to her aid. They had a surgeon on staff. They would help her.

A wheezing croak came from the floor beside me, and I looked down to see Morgan's laugh. Nothing remained in me then but black rage. I was on him, pummeling him with blow after blow. I knew a hundred ways to kill a man, but this, this wasn't going to be an easy death. I was senseless, beating and bashing without thought or reason until I was empty. A shell. And I became aware of a hand on my shoulder.

Morgan was unconscious, blood bubbling from his nose in small, weak puffs. But that was not what stopped me. It was the blood on Brendan. It was Brianna's blood.

It was a reminder. She had said my brother must live. To keep the rest of us safe, Morgan could not die.

I lifted a shaky hand to my chest, wiping the dampness as I surveyed the room. Emily was gone. Morgan's men were struck dumb, staring fixedly at the unmoving body beneath me. They had to know. Once Morgan had released them, they had to understand they'd been under his power.

"Go home," Brendan said weakly. "Go home and we will work this out tomorrow. Aern," he murmured as he wrapped a hand around my bicep to pull me to standing, "come on, you're injured."

I glanced down, surprised to find the knife wound in my side. I'd not even felt it.

Brendan's gaze fell to Seth and Eric, and he gestured with a jerk of his head for them to tend to the others.

"Wesley," he called, searching the room until he spotted the boy's red mop, "Brianna said she'd instructed you on dealing with Morgan."

"Yes, sir," he said. I thought he seemed somehow taller, but I was leaning heavily on Brendan now.

"Then get to it," Brendan said. "We've got a secure room on the lower level. It looks like he's out, but make sure no one touches him."

Wesley nodded. "Absolutely."

He rushed toward Morgan, calling orders to several other men for assistance, and I glanced at Brendan.

He shrugged. "Beats me. I'm just doing as I was told."

I coughed, and it tasted of copper.

"Right," Brendan said, "let's get you some rest."

When I woke, Emily was at my bedside, hand wrapped loosely in mine. I blinked, and then jerked to sitting as the memories came back to me.

"Whoa," Emily murmured, moving to still me before I made it to my feet. "It's okay."

"Brianna—"

"She's fine." She pressed me back to sit on the edge of the bed before her. "She's resting. The doctor was able to stitch her up."

My shoulders fell. "Oh, Emily, I'm so sorry—"

She put her fingers to my lips and saw the sick horror in my eyes. I had stabbed her sister.

She brushed her hand over my forehead, leaning forward to leave a slow kiss in its wake. "There's nothing to forgive, Aern."

A nauseated groan came out as my forehead dropped onto her side and she pulled me to her, rubbing a hand over my hair until my arms wrapped around her. It wasn't until she shifted that I realized we weren't alone.

I drew back from her to question why there were men outside my door.

"Brendan wanted to speak with you as soon as you woke," she explained.

My brows drew together, and she stared at me like I was missing something obvious.

"To see what you wanted to do about the men."

"The men?"

She glanced at the door, then back to me. "Your men." Council.

I closed my eyes.

A full minute passed.

Emily whispered, "Aern?"

"Just. Just give me a minute," I said through a wince.

I heard the smile in her voice. "Well, don't take too long, it's nearly morning."

I opened one eye. "Tuesday?"

She looked confused for a moment. Nodded without much conviction. "Yeah, I think so."

I blew out a deep breath before standing. "Tell Brendan I will be down shortly," I said to the men waiting outside.

Emily began to step back from me, but I enfolded her tightly in my arms. "Tuesday?"

She waited.

"I have something for you." I kissed her, slow and deliberate, and when I finally pulled away, she blinked dazedly.

"Do I get this every Tuesday?" she asked.

I smiled. She'd forgotten her birthday. I would tell her later. After we'd seen Brianna. After the men were dealt with. After I knew everyone who'd been lost.

She saw the nausea rise up again, and tugged on my hand. "Come on, let's get some breakfast and take care of the men."

I walked with her through the halls, but drew to a stop as we approached a large picture window. The sun was coming up, spreading over the trees in waves of crimson and orange.

"It can wait a few minutes," I said, glancing at Emily as the light colored her cheeks.

She smiled, and we stood together as morning dawned.

We were linked. We had created the union, fulfilled the prophecy. Brianna was safe. Morgan was no longer a threat. There would be no war, because the Seven Lines were in my control.

We were going to live.

My chest eased where I'd not realized it had been bound, and I took a deep breath.

Emily looked up at me, her green eyes finally clear of the ceaseless worry over her sister, the prophecy, finally looking ahead to something else. Something unknown.

"What now?" she asked.

I sighed. "I guess we rule the world."

She glared at me and I gave her my best crooked smile as I pulled her tighter to my side.

More by Melissa Wright

The Descendants Series
Book One: Bound by Prophecy
Book Two: Shifting Fate
Book Three: Reign of Shadows

The Frey Saga
Book I: Frey
Book II: Pieces of Eight
Molly (a short story)
Book III: Rise of the Seven

Shattered Realms
King of Ash and Bone

www.melissa-wright.com

Made in United States
Orlando, FL
25 November 2023